TENT REVIVAL

BOOK ONE OF THE REBECCA MYTHOS

EDMUND STONE

RIVER REVIVAL PRESS

Tent Revival

Book One of the Rebecca Mythos

Copyright 2021 by Edmund Stone

Edited by Lyndsey Smith

Cover art by MIBLART

Dedication

To Mikel Stone, my love, my wife, and the one who kicks my ass every day to keep me going.

To my friends, Lowell Miller and Justin Boote, supporters, beta readers, and confidants both.

To all the people who made this book possible with their contributions of character. Gordon Clancy and Adam Rawlins, to name a few.

To all the people of the Write Practice, my writers group the first draft of this book was presented to. Especially the recently departed Des Dixon who loved reading the excerpts I posted weekly. I was fortunate to call him friend.

Finally, to the people of my hometown of Garrison, Ky. You all may never realize how much you contributed to this book, but hopefully, these pages will reveal some of it.

INTRODUCTION

What you are about to read started way back in 2016. I was a new writer then, and as I suppose many new writers do, I studied. Not only by posting to my writers' group, but by observing the things around me. This form of observation gave me lots of interesting ideas. I wrote them all down, realizing one day, I'd have enough material to put it all in a book, and here it is my first novel.

Now, if I've given you the idea this all magically jumped from my head and lay comfortably on the written page, then I've misled you. A crime I would never want to be accused of. Mostly because its untrue. It took me nearly five years to get it right after all. No, this book was a collection of quirky things I saw around me. All starting with a box at work near the central supply office. A sticker was taped to the side saying, Mixed Parts. After this, the what ifs emerged. What if that box was a bunch of body parts, hibernating away, and ready to strike? As you read these pages, you'll see with greater clarity where my mind wanders.

Once the idea was cemented in my head, the characters started forming. People I knew, some I didn't, all with something to contribute. A few of those people know who they are, and maybe I'll reveal them someday. But for now, we'll keep it in these pages. The rest of the story evolved from the environment. Most notably, where I live. The people and places I see every day. Of course, the names are changed to protect the innocent, but the hometown feel is there just the same. The locals and others who live in small towns, will get a sense of this, and I hope they laugh a little.

When I began to write I realized the book needed a villain. One people could hate and love as well. Sage was originally that guy, but he didn't completely fit the mold, so, Rebecca was born. The definition of the name is 'to tie' or 'to bind'. As you read, you'll see why the name is appropriate.

Finally, all my characters and places were ready to go, and I sat down to write the story. I finished the original rough draft in one month, during NANOWRIMO. Once I finished, I read over it and hated it. Looking back though, I realize it needed to sit on a shelve for a few years. Partly because I bit off too much. I wasn't quite ready for the undertaking this novel demanded. Fast forward a few years, the beginning of 2021 to be exact, and Tent Revival was ready to see the light. Not only was it ready, but I had ideas for expanding it into an entire series. So, what you're reading is Book One of the Rebecca Mythos. I chose Mythos instead of series due to Rebecca is more myth than reality. Unfortunately for those who she comes for, she is all too real.

An entire series of books, all spawned from two common words. Funny how the mind of a writer works. I hope you enjoy this book. I sure enjoyed writing it. There will be others soon. You, my readers, are just getting started.

Thank you so much for spending your time here, and when you're finished, be sure to leave a review of what you thought of this book. I'd love to hear from you.

Edmund Stone
July 2021

Chapter One

Allen

S y Sutton sat in the parking lot of Lexington State Mental Hospital, staring at the red-orange clouds above the hills. It reminded him of what he used to say to his children: *Red sky at night, a sailor's delight; red sky at morn, and a sailor takes warn.*

It meant a storm was brewing, possibly a bad one. He wondered if it was a sign. Should he turn back?

His son Allen lay in a hospital bed in there, and the boy needed him. He couldn't leave when he was so close to seeing him again.

The past year had been crazy since his wife died, and he'd lost touch with his son. The odd thing was that Allen's wife died too, almost a year to the day. The accident that put him in the hospital happened after her funeral. It was all too much. If he could bring him home, care for him there, things would be different. They could bond again.

He reached inside his jacket pocket, fumbling for the small flask of liquor he'd filled before he left. The cheap stuff he brought from home was better than any you'd find in the stores.

It was eight thirty, time for visiting hours to begin. He placed the flask back into his jacket, took a deep breath, and got out of his car.

The hospital doors slid open, and he entered the main foyer. A guard sat at the desk along with a woman in a suit outfit. Another guard passed by on his way to the guard shack.

"Can I help you, sir?" the woman said.

"I'm here to see Allen Sutton. I'm his father, Sy Sutton."

"Okay. Let me check to see what room he's in." She looked at her computer. "Here he is, Room 311. The nurse on the floor will have to give you access; I'll tell her you're coming."

"Okay, thanks." Sy nodded and walked toward the elevator doors.

A pit formed in his stomach as he realized he was nervous about the meeting. His daughter, Sally, visited Allen a few days before. She told him he didn't look good and to be prepared.

As Sy exited the elevator, a pretty nurse—looking to be in her early forties, Sy guessed—greeted him. She wore sensible khakis with a button up blouse, her hair pulled back in a tight ponytail.

"Hello, sir. I'm the head nurse, Patty Hudson. You're Allen Sutton's father, right?"

"Yeah, but Sy's fine," he said as he put his hand out.

She shook it lightly. "Okay, would you like to see your son now?"

"Yes, please."

"He's in Room 311. Rhonda? I'm taking Mr. Sutton back to see his son. I'm leaving you in charge of the desk."

A red-haired girl with green eyes, looked up from the nurse's station, smiled, and nodded to Patty.

Patty walked stiffly to the door and punched a code into a keypad beside the glass barricade. She held the door open for Sy.

As Sy walked down the corridor, he felt like he was in another world. Strange noises came from the hall, screams and moans, things that didn't seem quite human.

He could see Room 311 up ahead. The door was closed, but the one before it was open.

A man sat on the bed with only a gown gaping open in the back. He faced the corner, murmuring to himself. The ridges of the man's spine protruded like some prehistoric creature, the skin taut around it looking dry and leathery. Red, scaly patches coated him from head to toe. The man looked older than his years would suggest, like a young man in an old man's body.

The ferocity of his movement increased as the murmurs began to turn into words. He spoke with an accent Sy had heard before, one of those British comedies or maybe Irish. It was hard to tell as his words were coming faster, building to a fevered pitch.

"From Earth it comes, to the dirt it returns...to the dirt it returns. From the Earth it comes, to the dirt it returns!"

The man snapped his head around and looked at Sy. His eyes were glassy, and the irises looked like they were swimming in milk. Pock-marks dotted his face with the same redness as the splotches, appearing as craters on his sunken cheeks. "Take the child away from here. For she seeks to destroy the womb, but the child, the child lives on...lives on! Lives on! Lives on!"

The man lunged for him.

Sy pedaled backward, colliding with Patty, sending them both crashing into the opposite wall.

Hurried footsteps came from the direction of the nurse's station.

"Harley!" Rhonda said, pulling a syringe from her pocket. There were two orderlies with her, and they grabbed Harley, pushing him against the wall. Rhonda deposited the contents of the syringe into his arm. He quit squirming almost immediately. The orderlies eased the wild man onto his bed.

"Bill, Nate, thank you," Patty said.

Harley smiled at Rhonda. "Thanks, my sweet." He then curled into a fetal position on the mattress.

"Please, Mr. Sutton. This way." Patty had collected herself and was motioning for Sy to follow. "I'm sorry about that. I'm not sure why his door was open."

She punched in a code below the handle and opened the door to 311. The room was small with a bathroom in the back. Allen lay sleeping in a hospital bed near the middle with monitors surrounding him. An IV was hooked to his arm and a tube stuck in his nose. His wrists and ankles were strapped to the bed like some heathen animal.

"Why's he being pumped full of dope? Isn't it counterproductive?"

Patty shook her head with a tight smile. "Allen's on a slow drip of Ativan. It's hardly dope. It keeps his heart rate normal and helps him to stay calm. Without it, he's prone to seizures. We're trying to make your son as comfortable as possible. Rest assured; he's well cared for."

"Yeah, I guess. I haven't talked to him for a few months, since before the accident. It's a little hard to see him this way. Why're his arms and legs strapped down?"

"Those are for his safety. If he woke while in seizure, he could fall from the bed before anyone got to him. A little archaic, but effective. I'll leave you to visit."

She studied the IV bag before she left. "Looks like this needs to be refilled. Rhonda should've replaced it an hour ago. I'll be back in a minute."

Sy held Allen's hand, squeezing it from time to time to see if he could get a response from him, but Allen made no sign he was even in the world. He sat back in the chair and then reached for his flask again. He unloosed the cap and took a drink, pausing as the warm liquid trickled down his throat.

He thought about why Allen was here. So much had happened in such a short time. Sadie, his wife of thirty years, passed, and Allen was near death himself. The boy had fallen into the sinkhole in town. He'd been in a coma ever since they found him. Sy knew he was distraught after his wife died but didn't think he would wander off and end up hurt. Nicole was good to Allen, and no one could understand why she'd commit suicide the way she did, not even her good-for-nothing family. They probably blamed Allen for the whole thing.

The sinkhole didn't seem to be getting any smaller either. The damned thing was going to swallow the whole town eventually. Sy had a lot to ponder while he watched his son's slow breathing. *Maybe if Allen heard his dad's voice, then he'd have a better chance of waking.*

He fished around in the top drawer of the bedside table and pulled out the Gideon's Bible left there. He cleared his throat and read a few verses. The story of Lazarus seemed especially appropriate for the situation.

As he read, he thought about his late wife, Sadie, how he believed strongly in the Bible while she was alive. But since she'd passed, he had a hard time with it, ignoring pleas from his daughter to come to church. He still remembered quite a bit but didn't have the conviction he once had. Maybe he'd lost his faith, or maybe he was just lost? The latter was probably true, but even though that may be, his faith was strong in his son.

Then, another thought occurred to him. When Allen woke up, what would he say to him? He hadn't spoken with anyone much over the course of the year. After Sadie died, Sy had practically been a recluse. He only left the house to meet up with his friend Buck for some of the corn alcohol he'd become so fond of.

He placed the flask in his pocket and watched Allen. If not for the occasional beep of the monitor, Sy would think the boy was dead. But in some ways, maybe he was. If only he could talk to him, like he'd wanted to for the last year. But all he had was the shell of a man, the once vibrant boy who couldn't stop talking when he was a kid.

Defeated, he sat back in his chair and looked out the window. It was so darkly tinted that all he could see was his reflection. It seemed like he'd aged twenty years in one week. Ever since Allen ended up there, he'd been on edge. His beard showed the evidence of how hard it had been on him; the gray had multiplied overnight, more than his fifty-five years should show.

"I need to get you out of here, son."

Suddenly, Allen bucked at the restraints and banged his head on the mattress. Veins protruded from his temples and arms, a network of blue running like road maps on his body. Sy rose from the chair, placing his hand on his son's arm.

"Allen? Allie? Are you awake?"

Allen relaxed a moment, turning his head toward his dad. The pupils in his eyes were starting to dilate, no longer the small black pinpoints they once were. The drugs were starting to lose their effect. He was coming back to consciousness.

"Hunmm...?" he said with a raspy voice.

"Allie, it's me; it's Dad. Wake up."

"Daa...d, wha...?"

"It's okay, Son. Save your strength. We don't have a lot of time."

"Dad, Dad is it...is it, really you?"

"Yes, Son. You're not dreaming. I'm here for you." Sy held Allen's hand in his.

"Dad, I'm thirsty."

"Oh, give me a second."

Sy studied the room. In the corner on a bedside table sat a pitcher of water with a straw in it. Sy brought it to him. He put his hand behind

Allen's head and gently lifted. Allen coughed as he drank from the straw.

"Take it easy. You've been out for a while. The only water you've been getting is from that damn needle in your arm."

"Dad, I'm sick." Allen cried, dropping his head on Sy's shoulder.

Sy fought back tears, as he stroked his son's face. "It's okay. I should have been there for you. But don't worry, I'll make it up to you. I'm getting you out of here. You hang in there."

"Dad? I love you." Allen looked at Sy, his eyes still trying to focus. "What's happening to me?"

"You're going through a bad spell, but it's going to be okay. I'm going to take you home."

"Home?"

"Yes. My home, where you were raised, Allen. This'll all be over soon. Then you can start living again."

Kissing his son on the forehead, he straightened and stepped into the hallway. A wheelchair stood against the wall between Harley's room and his son's. Sy hurriedly brought it inside the room and quietly shut the door again. He searched the drawers for a pair of socks and an extra pair of linen pants. With moderate difficulty, he was able to somewhat dress Allen, who had fallen back under.

A loud thump reverberated on the wall that separated his son's room from Harley's. Noises were coming from next door, and he could hear a commotion building in the hallway.

Allen moved slightly, his head gently rolling from side to side. Sy removed the wrist restraints. The skin was red and irritated from the straps, and he tried to soothe the area the best he could by rubbing gently.

The sounds coming from next door were getting louder and the conversation more heated. He paid no attention to it and removed the feet restraints. Then, with trepidation, he began to remove the nose tube. Once it cleared his nostril, Allen immediately started gagging. Sy rolled him to his side and grabbed the trash can by the bed, placing it under Allen's chin.

"Go ahead, Son. It's your body's way of rejecting the poison."

Allen emptied the contents of his stomach, all liquid and nothing solid, then rolled onto his back and groaned. Outside the room, the noise was reaching a fevered pitch with people yelling. Bill and Nate could be heard the loudest. Sy left Allen's side for a moment and went to the door. He peered into the hall. No one was there. The noises were coming from Harley's room.

Sy retrieved a small wash basin from the nightstand near the bed and placed it in Allen's hand.

"Here, keep this close in case you have to throw up again. We're getting out of here, now."

Allen's eyes rolled back, showing the whites. Sy wasn't sure how much he understood or how much help he would give getting into the wheelchair. Another loud thump hit the wall, causing a picture to tilt.

Harley must be giving them hell over there, he thought. The voices next door were louder and more desperate.

"Hold him down!" Nate cried out.

"I'm trying for fuck's sake! He's too strong!" Bill said.

Now was the best time to make his move, while they were distracted. He unfolded the wheelchair and placed it by the bed. He remembered how the Home Health Therapist for Sadie taught him to transfer someone from a bed to a wheelchair. Hopefully, Allen had enough strength to stand on his legs and help.

Awkwardly, he pulled his son to a sitting positioning on the edge of the bed, a little too forcefully, losing his balance and falling into him.

He steadied himself, grabbing Allen under the shoulders. *Let's see what this old man is made of*, he thought, then knelt as low as he could and tried to pull him to standing. Allen's legs bent when he tried to bear weight on them, and Sy, seeing his son wasn't going to stand, sat him back on the bed.

"All right, Allen, we'll have to do this the hard way."

With every bit of strength Sy could muster, he heaved his son into the wheelchair, slinging him like a sack of potatoes. But, as Allen's bottom touched the edge of the wheelchair, it immediately went sideways.

Damn, I forgot to lock the brakes!

He couldn't get Allen back to the bed, and the wheelchair was out of reach. So, he did the only thing he could and lowered him to the floor in a sitting position, gently leaning him against the bed. Sy had started to reposition the wheelchair when he noticed blood pouring down Allen's arm. In his haste, he'd forgotten to unhook the needle for the IV.

Shit, what was I thinking?

He took a pillowcase from the bed and wrapped it tourniquet-style around the bleeding wound on his son's arm. Sy repositioned himself, placing his hands under his son's shoulders again. Then, he squatted as low as possible and lifted Allen into the wheelchair with a grunt. Once Allen was situated, Sy let out a long breath and stretched, feeling his back pop.

Another loud thump hit the wall, and Sy heard male and female voices on the other side. *Time to go.*

He placed Allen's feet on the foot pedals of the wheelchair, then moved toward the door. He opened it and saw the hallway was clear. All the other rooms were closed, except for Harley's. He'd have to be quick, so no one would see them.

Sy pulled Allen and the wheelchair backward into the hall, then straightened and pushed forward. Loud shouting blared from the open room.

"She's coming! From the ground! She can't be buried forever!" Harley screamed.

It was time to get the hell out of there, but a voice came from beside him, sending shivers up his back.

"Mr. Sutton? Where do you think you're going with my patient?"

Sy could see Patty in the doorway to Harley's room. Her hair was messed up, and she didn't look as neat and tidy as she did earlier. "Listen, lady, I'm taking him out of here, even if I have to go through you," Sy said.

Patty stood her ground, but she and Sy both were distracted by the riotous turmoil going on next to them. Bill and Nate were barely holding Harley down, and Rhonda was wavering in her attempts to inject the needle in his leg. He had restraints on his ankles, but his strength was incredible, and he was beginning to get free.

"Hold him still!" Rhonda cried out.

Sy smiled. The distraction was well timed. "It looks like you have bigger problems in there."

"It can wait." She blew a piece of fallen hair from her face. "You don't understand what you're doing. I know you think you're trying to save him, but all you're doing is making things much worse. If Allen were awake, he'd agree with me."

"Well, he's not really in control now is he? Sometimes father knows best."

"We'll see about that. I'm calling security. They will have you apprehended before you get out the door." Patty turned toward the desk, but before she could take a step, a cry came from Harley's room.

"Forget it. I can't hold him anymore," Rhonda cried.

Patty turned toward the room and hesitated. "Stay right there."

Sy started to move past her, and she stepped in front of him.

"I'm warning you," she said.

Harley's broke free from his ankle restraints and came rushing toward the door, dragging Nate with him. Rhonda was knocked onto her bottom, the needle flying from her hand into the air. Bill attempted to stop him but was spun sideways into the wall. Nate fell to the wayside just as Harley stepped over the threshold.

Harley rushed headlong into the hallway, catching Patty in the mid-section. She screamed as he bit into her shoulder, pulling a bloody hunk of flesh free. Sy was too startled to move. Harley dropped Patty to the floor, and she crawled into the corner, whimpering. The crazy man looked at Sy with cataract-glazed eyes, only a thin circle of blue left around them, and spit the piece of skin from his mouth. Blood dripped from his chin and ran down his stubbly neck.

"The queen is rising. She will look for a new lover. Her flesh for yours." He turned his head toward Allen, grinning, blood running through his crooked, yellow teeth. "Are you worthy? Go to her! Go to her!" he screamed, splashing blood on Sy's shirt.

Sy eased backward from the man, but surprisingly, Harley stepped to the side to let them pass. Sy continued down the hall as Harley watched with an unnerving calm. Sy felt sorry for Patty lying on the floor, but just for a moment. It was time for him and Allen to go.

Surprisingly, the door at the end of the hall leading to the nurse's station and elevators was open. The nurses hadn't locked it back when they went to deal with Harley. It was almost too easy. Sy didn't dwell on it; he kept going, pushing Allen to the elevator doors. When they opened, he entered, taking one more glance down the hall.

As the doors closed, he caught a glimpse of Harley being tackled by Bill and Nate.

Chapter Two

The Great Escape

The darkness lay out like a velvet blanket on either side of the road. They were an hour out of Lexington, driving along I-64, still another good hour from home. It had been easy-going once they left the hospital. Sy had made one stop for fast food before getting on the interstate, but Allen slept through it while he ate. The exit from the hospital lot was surprisingly smooth as well. No security bothering them and no police, except for one incident while still in Lexington.

Not far from the hospital, a city patrol car trailed them, getting very close as though trying to read the license plate number.

Then, strangely, an old model Cadillac, painted black with silver wheels, came from nowhere. Sy noticed it right away, thinking it odd how it stood out, like the kind of car you'd see in an old presidential cavalcade. It pulled from an alleyway as he passed, then drove up beside him in the opposite lane, ignoring the cop car behind them.

Looking over, Sy tried to see the driver, but the windows were tinted so dark that nothing inside could be seen. The word Fleetwood stood out in chrome on the front fender. It hovered there momentarily, then slowed until even with the cop. Blue lights flashed, and Sy watched with interest as the Cadillac pushed the patrol car toward the sidewalk. There was a crunch of metal and tires screeching as the police car veered sideways off the road, hitting a streetlight hard enough to disable it.

Afterward, the Cadillac drove up beside Sy again and remained there for a moment. He gripped his steering wheel, ready for anything. But nothing happened. The big black car sped up and disappeared on a side street.

Sy nervously drove the rest of the way to the interstate with no new pursuers. Maybe everyone was after the Cadillac now, no longer interested in the old man who broke his comatose son out of a mental hospital. Sy wasn't sure but was happy to be on the way home. There were several eighteen wheelers out, clipping along at a steady speed, making up time before the next haul. He paced himself behind them until he saw the Morehead exit ahead, a place he knew well. His daughter went to college there.

Slowing to veer onto the exit, he glanced at Allen who was still sleeping, his head laying against the door. Sy figured Allen would sleep for a few days, then they'd have to deal with the withdrawal symptoms. He'd seen neighbors go through it with their loved ones. It was ugly, like exorcising a demon.

Sy took a left, drove for about a mile, then took a right onto State Route 377, taking them back to Salt Flat. The road wound for about forty miles to the North, some of the most remote areas in the state, nothing but hills and valleys. A few houses littered the large swaths of farmland and timber laying out to either side of the snaking highway.

It was late in the evening, and darkness enveloped the scenery around them. A thick fog rolled in, clinging to the valley, making visibility tougher. Slowing to a crawl, Sy squinted to see the road in front of him.

Suddenly, light illuminated the cloud bank, and he saw a pair of headlights coming straight at him. He slammed the brakes with no time to swerve, sending Allen lunging forward before being locked in by the seatbelt, his head bouncing against the seat with a thump. He moaned but didn't wake up.

"What the hell?" Sy looked through the windshield into the fog ahead, his hands still shaking.

But there was nothing, no sign of a car or anything, only the pea soup surrounding him.

Easing his foot off the brake, he drove slowly. Out of nowhere, he heard the unmistakable roar of a large V8 engine. Headlights shone in the rearview for a moment before veering to the side in the opposite lane. Pulling up beside him was the Cadillac from earlier. It revved its engine a few times and settled to a low rumble.

The whole thing was unnerving, the stranger's car driving in the other lane. What if another car came? Sy lowered his window and attempted to see the driver, but the glass on the Cadillac was so dark that all he could see was his own reflection. The Caddy revved its engine again, so loud Sy thought he would have ear damage.

"Who the hell are you?" Sy shouted.

The car lunged forward, pulling in front of Sy's car. Instinctively, he hit the brakes, nearly veering off the road. He momentarily saw the taillights as the car disappeared into the fog.

"Asshole," Sy whispered.

The fog lifted as quickly as it came on, leaving only the darkness. A car passed, going normal speed. Shaking his head, Sy felt as though they had been in another dimension for a moment, like one of those Twilight Zone episodes he liked to watch years before. Even though he was glad for the assist back in the city, he wished to never see that Caddy again. Hopefully, the rest of the trip would be uneventful.

"Damned peculiar," he said.

Chapter Three

Close to Home

It was near 1:00 a.m. when they reached Salt Flat, and everything was quiet. A few cars belonging to the night shift workers who carpooled to jobs in the next county over remained in the lot at McDonald's, belonging to the night shift workers who carpooled to jobs in the next county over. In Salt Flat, the sidewalks were rolled up and put away around 8:00 p.m. Anything happening beyond that time was behind closed doors or out at the bar on the edge of the county.

Sy heard Allen gagging and glanced over. Pulling off the road, Sy waited while Allen opened the door, heaved, and emptied the contents of his stomach on the ground. Giving him time finish, Sy asked, "Are you okay, Allie?"

"I think so, but I'm cold and hurting everywhere." Sweat pooled on Allen's pallid skin, and he was shaking all over like he was running a fever.

Placing the back of his hand on Allen's forehead, Sy felt for a temperature. Allen's skin was clammy, but he wasn't too hot. Sy grabbed his jacket from the back seat and laid it over him.

"There, that'll keep you warm. You're going to be fine. Your body is trying to get rid of the poison. That's all." Sy tried his best to be reassuring.

Moaning, Allen gathered the jacket around his body, closed his eyes, and lay back against the seat. Sy pulled the car back onto the road and, drove for home. Once he got Allen in his house, all would be better.

They were about three miles from home when Sy noticed a large canvas tent erected at the edge of the woods near Bill and Myrtle Owens' farm. It was a peculiar sight and unnerving, the canvas edges fluttering lightly in the breeze, the weathered white fabric a stark contrast to the dark woods behind it. He hadn't seen a tent like that one in years, since he was a kid. Slowing to a crawl to get a better look, his headlights shined on a sign by the edge of the road with large red letters printed on it.

Come join us Friday night for a Tent Revival.
Preaching and evangelism provided by the Sage.

There was no preacher around there named Sage. Sy wondered if Pastor Mooney at First Methodist knew about it. Strange, but stranger still was to see anything parked at the Owens' farm. They didn't take kindly to strangers, and they sure didn't like their farm messed with.

Speeding up slightly and keeping his eyes on the road the best he could, Sy tried to see as much of the tent as possible while they passed. A car sat parked on the other side, one he recognized immediately. It was the Cadillac he'd encountered in Lexington and on the road home; he was sure of it.

"Damned peculiar," he said aloud.

"What, Dad?" Allen raised his head and wincing in discomfort.

"Nothing, just rest. We'll be home soon."

Sy turned into East Side Trailer Park, the place he called home. He passed four trailers and pulled into his driveway on the left, but it wasn't empty. Sally's car was there.

Normally, Sy wouldn't think anything of his daughter being at the house, but at one thirty in the morning, it could only be about one thing—Allen. She sat on the front porch with a scowl on her face, and Sy prepared for a lecture. He put the car in park and opened the driver's door. Sally met him as he stepped out.

"Dad! What were you thinking?" She crossed her arms under her breasts, her bosom heaving with each frustrated breath.

"I've been on the phone with the doctor and head nurse of the hospital. They want to know why you took Allen against medical advice. For Christ's sake, Dad, he's sick!"

"Now, Sally. You didn't see him there. You didn't see the poison they were putting in him." Sy shook his head.

"I've been trying to call you. Don't you have your cell phone with you?"

Patting his pocket, knowing it wasn't there, Sy shrugged.

She hesitated, taking a deep breath. "No, of course you don't."

"It's in the bedroom on the nightstand."

"No surprise. I'll bet you had the flask with you though."

While they were arguing, the passenger door opened, and Allen leaned out, heaving. Noticing her brother's distress, Sally ran to him. She was taken aback by his appearance. The hospital gown barely clung to the top of his body, and the pants hung loosely over his thin legs. His pallid color made him look like a ghost. Blood seeped down his arm all the way to his wrist.

"Allen? Are you okay? My God, you should be under the care of a doctor."

"Well, he's here now, Sally. Could you help me get him in the house?"

"Okay, Dad. But this is crazy. What if he dies?"

"He's not going to die. Now help me out."

Placing their arms under Allen's shoulders, they lifted him to standing. Instinctively, he grabbed for them to steady himself. With his arm around her neck, Sally placed her other arm around his waist. Sy held him up on the other side, and on wobbly legs, Allen stepped forward toward the house.

They managed to get him onto the couch, and Sy found a light blanket to cover him with. Allen curled into a fetal position, and Sally tucked the blanket around him the best she could.

"I'll get the spare bedroom ready." Sy walked down the hallway. Moments later, after a few bangs and curses, he stepped back into the small living room. "I've got the bed ready, Sally. Can you help me get him in there?"

Sally knelt beside her brother, and with her dad's help, they wrestled him into the bedroom that had once been her mother's hospice room. Once he was in bed with blankets covering his whole body, she motioned for Sy to meet her in the hall.

"My God, what happened to him? I can't believe how much he's changed."

"It was that place and the drugs they kept feeding him. He'll get better now."

"Daddy? Do you know how to take care of someone detoxing?"

"I took care of your mother, didn't I?"

"Yes, you did, and she was bad, but all you had to do was follow the hospice nurse's instructions. This is a whole different thing. Also, Mom was dying and only needed comfort care measures. Allen's not dying, but he could if not properly taken care of. I had a friend who detoxed from pain killers, and I can tell you, it wasn't easy. Did you find out what they were giving Allen in the hospital?"

"No, it was on an IV pole and fed to him by a slow drip. The nurse said the name of it several times, but I'm not good with that stuff. They also gave him injections when he got rowdy. I think it was called Ativon or Ativan, something like that."

"Ativan, I've heard of it. They use it to calm people. I can only imagine how much was in the IV. The injections were probably something much stronger." She sighed. "He's going to have a hard time coming off all of it."

"Will you help me, Sally? I may have bitten off more than I can chew, but he's my kid. I would do the same for you."

"I know, Dad. I can't believe I'm getting involved in this. If it weren't family, I wouldn't. We'll try to get in touch with an agency later today. For now, we'll keep an eye on him. I'll call a sub in for work, so I can take the day off. I'll tell them it's a family emergency. They'll understand. I'll call Tom and let him know."

Watching as she dialed the phone, Sy wondered how ole Tom would take it all this. He and Sy never saw eye to eye on much of anything, so he figured it wouldn't go well. Tom was your typical Friends of the NRA, gun-wielding redneck from these parts. Sy, who owned a gun also but never used the damn thing, thought the NRA was a gimmick, trying rather successfully to funnel money, scaring them with how the president, whoever it was, was going to take everyone's guns and declare Marshall law. Biggest bunch of horse shit he'd ever heard, but Tom fed into it and a host of other half-baked ideas.

If Tom wasn't inconvenienced in any way, he probably wouldn't worry about what was going on with Allen. But with Sally wanting to help, Sy knew things could get rocky. Hopefully, Tom would stay out of it, but Sy figured he'd have to deal with him at some point.

"Okay, all set with Tom. I'll call work in a few hours."

"Tom was okay with it? I'm surprised."

"Dad, you two are always at each other. I guess another man can never take the place of a girl's dad, now can they?"

"You said it," Sy said smiling.

"All right then, you go to your room and try to get some sleep. I'll stay here with Allen in case he wakes and needs anything."

"Sally, I appreciate all you're doing. It's good to have your help."

"It's no problem. We'll try to get help, but Dad, if we can't, you need to be ready to send him back to the hospital for treatment."

"We'll cross that bridge when we get there," he said with the best non-committal tone he could muster.

"Okay, Dad, get some sleep and keep your cell close."

Chapter Four

The Prodigal Son

Sy's dreams were being invaded as he restlessly tried to sleep. In them, he saw Allen being dragged into a dark hole. Something from within, a darkness, swallowed him as Sy screamed for his son. He woke shaking.

The stress of getting Allen home seemed to be taking its toll. The clock radio on the nightstand read 6:00 am. Shuffling half asleep to the bathroom, he emptied his bladder, then made his way to the kitchen. Opening the refrigerator, he reached for what was left of the milk. He took a drink and the cold liquid hitting his belly instantly satisfied him.

He left the lights out, relying instead on the small glow of morning light peeking through the blinds as the July sun began to rise outside. It offered enough luminescence for him to navigate through the small trailer.

Pushing the spare bedroom door open slightly, he saw Allen covered in a layer of blankets and Sally stretched out in the reclining chair next to the bed. It was good to have them both home at the same time. Sy couldn't remember the last time they were there together.

He smiled and returned to the kitchen. There wasn't much to offer in the way of food: the half-gallon of milk, a loaf of bread, and some lunch meat nearly past its guaranteed freshness date. There were a couple of bottled waters and condiment containers older than him. If he was going to feed Allen, he needed to do some grocery shopping soon.

He hadn't been to the IGA down the street in a while. Truth be told, since Allen had been in the hospital, he found himself drinking more than eating. But those days were over; it was time to straighten up for Allen's sake.

He grabbed a bottle of water and went back to the bedroom, feeling sleep coming on him again.

Good, because he would need all the rest he could get.

While Sy slept, a car pulled up outside. It was a Cadillac, the kind you'd see in an old presidential cavalcade. A pretty girl with red hair and green eyes stepped out, holding a large handbag. Boldly, she walked up to the door of Sy Sutton's house. The Cadillac sped off and Rhonda Lane, sat her handbag down, straightened her skirt, then knocked.

Sy woke to a knock on the door. He rubbed his eyes to adjust and looked at his clock. It read eight thirty. Dropping his legs over the side of the bed, he put his feet in his house shoes and stood. Sy saw his reflection in the mirror on the opposite side of the room and licked his fingers, trying to tame the wild mess of hair on his head.

Stumbling from the bedroom, he reached for the front door, turning the knob, and pulling it open with one hand while still trying to mat his hair down with the other.

He peered at the girl on the front porch and had to blink twice.

"Rhonda? What are you doing here?"

"Hey, Mr. Sutton."

"You can call me Sy."

"Sy…How's Allen doing?"

"Fine. He's sleeping. What are y—"

"Dad? Who's at the door? Is it Tom?" Sally called from the spare bedroom.

Closing the door slightly and placing his head behind it so not to scream in Rhonda's face, Sy called to Sally. "No. Could you come here, please?"

Sy smiled at Rhonda. "Do you want to come in?"

"Sure."

As Rhonda walked through the door, Sally came out of the bedroom, pulling at her clothing, trying to look presentable.

"Hey, Sally, I want you to meet Rhonda Lane. She was one of Allen's nurses at the hospital."

Sally looked at Sy inquisitively before extending her hand to Rhonda. "A nurse, huh? I don't remember seeing you when I visited, Allen. My name's Sally Chambers. I'm Allen's sister. Nice to meet you."

"Yes, I was hired on a few days before Sy came to the hospital. Allen told me he had a sister. Nice to meet you as well."

"So, you knew Allen?" Sally said.

"Yes, we were friends and worked together before his accident. I knew Nicole, too. We all hung out after work. You know, health care workers. The job's stressful, so it's good to hang out with like-minded people and unwind."

"And what brings you to our neck of the woods?" Sy said.

"Well, if it's not too bold, I'm looking for a job."

Turning their heads as if they were thinking the same thing—and probably were—Sy and Sally smiled.

"Funny you should say that, because Dad and I were talking earlier about Allen needing a nurse for his care. We didn't expect one to just fall in our laps."

"Well, here I am. I hated the hospital and the way they treated Allen and Harley."

"Speaking of Harley, how'd Patty do after all the commotion last night?"

Sally broke in. "Who's Harley?"

"A patient who was next to Allen's room. A bit of a rowdy one too. He caused a big ruckus last night," Sy replied.

Rhonda continued. "Well, Patty took the day off, but not before chewing me out. I didn't mind. Harley needed me as well as Allen, and I was there. I'm kind of a self-made traveler, landing wherever I need to go. I only took the job because I knew Allen. I figured you were going to bring him home, so I came looking for him. I guessed, hoped, you would need a nurse, someone who can help while he's recovering from the drug load he was on. How's he doing so far?"

Sally smiled. "He's good, sleeping right now, although not a good sleep. He was restless, rolling around and yelling through the night."

Sy's brow furrowed, as he considered what Sally had said.

"Yelling, huh? What was he saying?"

"I'm not sure, gibberish mostly, talking about dirt, and, and..."

"A woman?" Sy finished.

"Yes, Dad, I think it was, something about the womb, or something crazy like that."

Sy thought about this, then said, "Sounds like the same babble Harley kept muttering. The drugs must be pretty heavy."

"Yes, they were. He was on a strong sedative. I was giving it to him every day intravenously, not to mention the benzodiazepine injections he was getting. Can I see him?" Rhonda asked.

Sy turned toward Allen's bedroom. "Right this way."

Sally stepped aside while her dad led the way into the spare bedroom. Rhonda followed them, adjusting her handbag onto her shoulder.

The appearance of the room embarrassed Sy, but he supposed much of it would come in handy for Allen. One corner was stacked with quilts and memorabilia and another with old electronic equipment and medical supplies he no longer used. Allen was even sleeping in Sadie's old hospital bed. Sy hadn't planned on keeping it, but he was thankful he did now.

"Sorry, the place is a wreck. This is where my wife spent her last days."

"I'm so sorry," Rhonda said.

"No, it's okay. Cancer took her from me a year ago." Sy motioned with his head toward Allen. "Enough about my wife; let's talk about him.

Sally smiled at Rhonda. "Yes, we're not sure how much it'll cost, but we're willing to make arrangements to pay what you need."

Sy nodded in agreement.

"Honestly, I don't need the money. Just a place to stay."

Sy shook his head. "Nonsense, we'll pay you. I'd rather it be you than someone Allen doesn't know."

"We'll discuss it later. Right now, I need to make sure Allen's okay."

Siting on the bed, Rhonda pulled the blanket away from Allen. She took a finger and pressed on his back above the scapula, leaving a thumb impression. The mark stayed white for a moment before becoming red. She reached into her bag, retrieving a pistol grip thermometer. Hovering the instrument an inch or two from his head, she waited for a beep, subtly shaking her head at the results.

Sy frowned. "What's wrong?"

"He's running a low- grade fever. Nothing out of the ordinary, just his system fighting the drugs. He'll be fine as soon as I get some fluids in him."

"Won't he have to go to the hospital for that kind of procedure?" Sally asked.

"No, not at all. I have fluid packs in my bag, saline and a few minerals, everything a growing boy needs to get back up and running. If I could get that IV pole in the corner, I'll hook him up now." Rhonda looked at the dried blood on the arm the old needle had been in. "We'll need to use the other arm. I doubt I could get another needle in the old site. It's way too irritated."

Sy retrieved the pole and placed it close to the bed under Sally's watchful eye. Rhonda seemed to notice Sally's inhibitions.

"It's all right. I'm here because Allen needs a nurse's care, one not working for the people who put him in this state." She smiled at both Sy and Sally.

Sy saw why Allen was friends with Rhonda. The infectious smile and no-crap attitude made her amiable. He liked her.

"Sy? Can you help me hold his arm? The good one."

Sy held Allen's limp arm while she inserted the IV and began the fluid drip. The bag of fluid had a red tinge to it, different looking than the ones Sy saw in the hospital. Those were clear.

He supposed it was because of the minerals Rhonda had mentioned. She massaged Allen's arm gently and stood, pulling the gloves loose from her hands and setting them in a pile with the discarded equipment wrappings.

"I'll take those," Sally offered.

"Thank you. Is there somewhere I can wash my hands?"

"Yeah, the spare bathroom is right around the corner." Sy pointed in the direction of the hallway. "Rhonda, I can't tell you how much I appreciate this. I guess I got ahead of myself when I took Allen from the hospital."

"I don't blame you. He needs to be home. They weren't taking care of him properly there."

Sy supposed he was justified in his decision, and the girl verified it. Allen was in good hands now.

Sally discarded the trash into a small wastebasket in the corner and handed it to Sy.

"Here, Dad, put this by the bed so she'll have a place to throw things away."

"Okay. She's great, isn't she?"

"Yes, she is. Just what we needed. Allen already looks better. I wonder what's in that stuff?"

"Just what the doctor ordered. Sally? You wouldn't want to go with me to the grocery store? I have house guests and nothing to feed them."

"Of course, Dad. Let me call Tom and give him the news. I talked to him last night when Allen first got home, and he's taking Eli to school. Since I have the day off, it won't be a problem getting you settled in."

Rhonda returned from the bathroom, drying her hands on her pants. "Sorry, I didn't see any towels in there."

"I suppose there aren't any. I need to get this bachelor's pad up to snuff." Sy chuckled.

"Come on, Dad, let Rhonda stay with Allen, and we'll get you stocked up."

"Okay. Is there anything I can get for you while I'm out, Rhonda?"

"Maybe some coffee. I'm not picky when it comes to food, so whatever is fine. I do like pumpkin flavored creamer, though."

"Consider it done. See you soon." Following Sally down the hall, Sy grabbed his coat and headed for the door.

Rhonda pulled back the curtain from the small bedroom window and watched as the car backed out of the driveway.

"Alone at last," she said. "I believe you could use a bath, Allen. What do you think?"

Allen made no response, only lay there sleeping, his back to her. She found a small plastic bath basin in the bathroom, the kind you get for free with your hospital stay and filled it with water. There were no towels or washcloths in the bathroom, so she used a pillowcase from a spare pillow.

Returning to the bedroom, Rhonda sat the basin on the nightstand. She studied Allen once the sheet was removed, pulling his pants off and throwing them in the corner. Slowly, she washed his upper body, paying close attention to under his arms and other areas more prone to sweating, and then to his feet, working her way methodically up his legs. She paused for a moment before washing his mid-section. His penis lay limp.

"Hmm, that won't do."

Lathering up the pillowcase with more soap, she stroked up and down his shaft. A small erection, not fully hard but responsive to her touch, formed in her hand. She took her clothes off. Continuing to massage and stroke with one hand, she used her other to touch herself until she was aroused. She orgasmed after a few motions.

Satisfied with her work, she crawled into the bed, easing her naked body next to Allen's. Placing an arm around him, she kissed him lightly on the back of his neck. Allen stirred and instinctively pressed his back into her as she cradled him.

"Oh, Allen. I've missed you so much. I need you to come back to me, baby. I know you won't remember what happened. But it's okay. We can start over here. This is a good place to begin. You'll see, we'll be happier than ever."

Chapter Five

Wake Up Allen

Sam's IGA sat in the middle of town, a regular stop for most of the residents of Salt Flat, the only grocery store for miles around. The big chain stores were thirty minutes away.

There weren't a lot of cars in the lot; it was a weekday, after all. On a weekend, the space to park was so small, you had to pull in across the street. Sam would usually be outside, directing people to not block the gas pumps. He was a portly man who didn't move fast and was comical to watch, especially if some kids were taunting him like they usually did.

They walked inside and saw Sam standing behind the cigarette counter. He caught Sy's eye and gave him a robust greeting.

"Hey, Sy," he said, then seeing Sally, waved to her too. "How you all doing?"

"Doing well, Sam," Sally said. "Do you still have the deli meat on sale?"

"Sure do. Nancy's over there. She'll set you right up."

"Dad? Why don't you go over and check it out? I'm going over to the produce section first. A girl as small as Rhonda, probably eats a lot of salad."

"I will." He lowered his voice so Sam couldn't hear. "There usually isn't much to choose from here. You have to go to the big chain stores to get the good stuff. Besides, what makes you think you know what Rhonda likes?"

"Dad, she said she wasn't picky, a nice way of saying, 'I like healthy stuff, but don't want to impose.'"

"Maybe you're right. At least I know where to find the one thing I was asked to pick up."

"Okay, you go to the dairy aisle. Go to the deli afterwards, and I'll meet you there."

"Okay, sounds good," Sy said, nodding at Sam as he walked past. Just ahead, a stock boy was sweeping the aisle.

"Hi, Mr. Sutton," he said.

"Hi, Johnny. Sam's keeping you busy, I see."

Once at the dairy section, Sy scanned the cooler next to the milk until he saw an orange-colored bottle. Pumpkin spiced latte.

"Aha, there you are."

Retrieving the bottle, he decided to check the coffee and tea aisle since he was right next to it. He was out of most everything at home, coffee included, and he figured nurses might be heavy coffee drinkers. He'd get some tea, too, just in case.

Perusing the aisle, he picked up a can of Columbian blend—not gourmet, but strong and smooth—then he grabbed a box of teabags. He juggled the items in his hands and thought he better get to the deli while he could still hold everything. As he started for the front of the store, he heard Sally talking to someone in the next aisle over. It sounded like Greta Oeny, the school secretary. Sy would know her irritating voice anywhere. It was as loud as the makeup she usually wore on her face. Stopping in the aisle, he leaned close to a shelf of cereal and listened to their conversation.

"Sally. How are you dear?"

"I'm fine, Greta. Just doing some grocery shopping for Dad."

"I heard Allen was back in town. How is he, after he fell in that hole?"

"How'd you know? He just came home last night?"

"Oh, you know how it is. Word gets around fast in this town."

"Apparently. He's doing better now, sleeping at Dad's house."

"Oh, is Sy taking care of him all by himself?"

"No, not entirely. We have a nurse staying there now. She's taking care of his medical needs."

"Oh. Are you paying her?"

"We have an arrangement. Greta, it's been good seeing you, but I have to get Dad's shopping done."

"Okay, but before you go, have you seen the big tent out at the edge of town?"

"No. What tent are you talking about?"

"It's one of those old circus-like tents, big and flappin' in the wind. Out by the Owen's farm. I drove by there this morning. There wasn't a soul around. A sign out front says there's a tent revival coming this Friday. The fella puttin' it on calls himself the Sage. Do you know he's already been to the school? He's a magician and has performed for the kids."

"The Sage? A magician? He sounds like an interesting person, but why haven't I heard anything about this?"

"I'm surprised you haven't. It's the talk of the town. Everybody knows about it. Tom doesn't let you out much, does he?"

"Everybody knows? How long's this thing been up?" Sally said, sounding surprised.

"I'm not sure, maybe yesterday. But the Sage was doing his magic show at the school a couple of days ago. He's quite the charmin' fella.

All dapper in his tuxedo suit and top hat. Your boy's in high school, isn't he? He should have seen the show."

"Yes, he is. I'll have to ask him about it when he gets home tonight."

"I hope he brings some pictures. You'll see what I mean about how handsome he is. That Sage could get some girls rauled up 'round here. If you know what I mean, grrr."

"I see. I'm sure he is, but my Tom's more than enough man for me."

"I would say the same thing about my Ralph, but just wait to you see the Sage. That's all I'm sayin'," Greta said with a raspy, cigarette-induced chuckle. "Are you going out there on Friday?"

"I don't know. I'll have to ask Tom first. Maybe."

"You'll change your mind when you meet him. Sam's got him coming here to the parking lot on the afternoon before the revival."

"Really? Right out here?"

"Yep. Ought to be a good time, supposed to be a concert with a Bluegrass band and everything."

"Wow, Greta, the town's putting up the welcome wagon for this stranger, aren't they?"

"They sure are, and for good reason. People like the Sage don't come around often. This place needs some cheerin' up, what with all the bad things the fake news is sayin' about us, drugs and poor people and all."

Just as Greta was going to go into another spiel, Sy rounded the corner, clumsily holding an arm full of groceries. Greta noticed him first. "Hey, Sy. How you been? Sally tells me you're going to have your hands full for a while, with Allen back and all."

"Yeah, I suppose so." He glanced at Greta and then turned to his daughter. "Sally, you 'bout ready to go?"

"Sure, Dad. Greta, I guess I better get Dad home."

"Sure, I'll see you at the tent, maybe? Tell Tom to come too."

"Maybe," Sally said.

Pushing her cart past them, Greta smiled and winked at Sy as she passed. Returning a nervous half-smile, he followed Sally to the front of the store, where he helped her empty the cart onto the checkout counter. Sy was overwhelmed with the variety of fruits and vegetables Sally had picked up, more than Sy would eat in a year. There were also several cans of chicken soup and a twenty-four pack of bottled water. He added the items he was holding as well.

"Dad? Did you get the deli ham?"

"Oops, forgot. I'll go over there right now."

"Okay, Dad, but slice it thin. Allen likes it that way."

On his way to the deli, Sy started thinking of something else he forgot, the thing only his friend, Buck Stanley, would possess. Home-grown moonshine, the perfect elixir for colds, a good sleep tonic to boot. Buck supplied the locals from his still over on Hackworth Hollow.

Sy paid for the meat at the deli counter, then met Sally at the front of the store. Johnny followed them out and helped unload the groceries. Once they were in the car, Sally started it, put it in reverse, and began to back out of the parking lot.

"Sally, what do you make of this Sage character?"

"So, you heard mine and Greta's conversation?"

"Every last bit. Greta ain't the quietest talker, you know? Do you think it's strange the entire town is welcoming this guy? I mean, Ralph Oeny is the sheriff, and his wife isn't even suspicious?"

"Well, Ralph and Greta ain't really that close these days. I heard she caught him in bed with another woman." Sally glanced sideways at Sy.

"If I had to listen to a woman like her all day, well, let's just say, some sins can be forgiven."

"Dad. Sin is sin, and you know it."

"I guess so." Sy looked out the window toward the road to Hackworth Hollow. "We need to get these groceries home. I have some other errands to run."

Sally shook her head, knowing what her dad had up his sleeve. "Do you mean, a visit to Buck Stanley's place? You know I don't like you going out there. I know you're picking up moonshine."

"It's for Allen. When he wakes up, he may need a good hot toddy."

She let out a sigh. "Okay, I guess. But I don't think it's a good idea to have shine around when you have a guest." She shook her head.

Pulling into the driveway to Sy's trailer, Sally stopped close to the porch to make it easier to unload the groceries. Sy opened the passenger door and walked around to the trunk of the car. Gathering two bags of groceries in his arms, he started for the house. As he stepped onto the porch, he saw Rhonda standing by the front door, holding it open for him.

"Need some help?" she said.

"I've got these, but Sally may need you. How's Allen?"

"Better. Why don't you ask him?"

Sy looked at her, surprised. "He's awake? Already?"

"Yep, sitting up in bed now."

Sy gave her a puzzled look, then smiled. "Wow, you are a miracle worker!"

Rhonda grinned sheepishly, then walked to Sally's car to help. Sy sat the groceries on the kitchen countertop and quickly made his way to the bedroom. He couldn't believe what he saw. There was Allen, sitting upright in bed.

"Hey, dad. How's things in the big metropolis of Salt Flat?"

Sy considered him for a moment, moisture forming in his eyes, before embracing Allen, pulling him close.

"Oh, son. I love you so much. I didn't think I'd ever talk to you like this again."

"Easy, Dad, it's okay. I'm all better, thanks to Rhonda."

Sy released his son from his embrace. "The prodigal son."

"What?"

"You're like the prodigal son who's returned. I don't have a fatted calf, but I bought chicken soup and some lunch meat from Sam's."

"Sounds great. I'm pretty hungry."

Sy thought it to be the most wonderful thing he'd ever seen. He jumped to his feet. "Absolutely. I'll be back in a second."

But before he could leave, Sally came through the door. "Allie! You're awake."

"Hey, sis. Come over here and give me a hug."

Tears of joy streaked Sy's faces. "I don't know how to thank you enough, Rhonda."

"It's no big deal. He needed fluids is all. Allen will be good as new in no time."

"Hey, Rhonda. Come with me to the kitchen. I'm going to fix Allie some soup and a sandwich."

"Sure, no problem at all. Lead the way. I'm right behind you."

Sally released her brother from her embrace. She noticed how well the color had returned to his skin. He looked as though he'd gained weight as well, not the gaunt specimen they left behind that morning. Strange that Allen could recover so quickly in just a few hours. *Whatever fluids Rhonda gave him must be powerful.*

"Allen? How do you feel? This morning you weren't even in this world. How did you make such a miraculous recovery?"

"I honestly feel great, Sal. Whatever Rhonda used on me did wonders."

"It was saline and special electrolytes, just what the doctor ordered." Rhonda said, walking in the room holding a bowl of chicken soup.

Sy, carrying a plate with a ham sandwich on it, followed behind her. He was also carrying a water bottle. Sally stood from the bed and allowed Sy to sit by Allen.

"Here you go, son. Eat slowly. I don't want you getting sick on me."

Allen ate the sandwich first, gobbling it down with no problem at all, and drank half the bottle of water before starting on the soup. Sy marveled at how he could eat, when he couldn't even keep water down the day before.

"My, son, you seem to have gotten your appetite back awfully quick. What's in that bag of goodies you put in his arm, Rhonda?" Sy asked.

"Like I said, saline and some electrolytes. They must be working."

"I'll say. You'll be back to your old self in no time, Allen."

Drinking the rest of the broth from the soup, Allen sat the bowl down and regarded Sy. "I'm better, Dad, because I have a good nurse. Rhonda? Can you help me get this needle out of my arm? I need to go relieve myself."

Sally stepped forward with a look of concern. "Rhonda? Is it a good idea to take him from the IV so soon?"

"He'll be fine for now. If he needs more solution, I can put everything back together easily enough." Rhonda skillfully released Allen from his intravenous drip, placing a cotton ball over the needle site. She taped it to keep it from falling off.

Allen threw his legs over the edge of the bed, stood, and stretched, raising his arms into the air. Sally and Sy's eyes widened when they noticed he had no clothing on. Rhonda grabbed a blanket from the bed and covered Allen with it.

"Oops, sorry. I had to give him a bath while you were gone and forgot to put clothes back on him."

Allen laughed. "It's no big deal. Dad and Sally have seen naked people before, I'm sure."

This is strange talk coming from Allen, Sally thought. He had always been private with those kinds of things growing up, hardly even letting their dad in the bathroom when he became a teenager.

Watching him walk across the room, Sally, over her initial shock, still couldn't believe it was Allen she was seeing. The transformation was amazing. He looked strong and vibrant, like nothing had ever happened to him.

"Allen? I think some of your old clothes are still here. When I saw you in the hospital, I wasn't sure if they'd still fit you or not, but seeing you now, I'm sure they'll be fine."

"Yeah, Dad. Sounds good. Can you bring them to me while I'm in the bathroom?"

"Sure, son."

Sy walked to the chest of drawers across the room and retrieved some clothing. He lay them on the bed, then turned to Sally.

"Can you help me put the rest of the groceries away?"

"I can help, too," Rhonda offered.

"No, you stay here for Allen. We can handle everything. Thank you though."

"Okay, I'll help him get into his clothing," she said.

Nodding in agreement, Sy left the room with Sally behind him. Once they were in the kitchen, he checked the hall to make sure no one was listening.

"Did you notice anything strange about Allen?" Sy said.

"Other than the fact he's recovered quicker than I thought possible and doesn't mind being in the buff?" she replied, sarcastically.

"Yeah, not the modest kid we knew. But more than that, he looks like a different person, full of color and smiling."

"He's different all right, Dad, but the good thing is, if he's recovering this quickly, you won't have to care for him long."

"I know, Sally. He was in a coma, for God's sake. Don't you think he should be worse?"

"Well, yes. I mean, I suppose. But you don't know. He may not have been as bad as you thought before. We should try not to think about it. Rhonda is taking good care of him and she's cute. They knew each other before. Maybe she knows things about him we don't."

"Maybe. They sure do seem cozy."

"Oh, Dad, she is a nurse. I'm sure she's given baths to lots of people."

"I guess it's a lot to take in. But, Sally, I know my son, and something about this isn't right. I wanted a miracle and I got one, but it seems strange is all."

"Granted, I think it's odd, too, but I'm sure everything's going to be okay, Dad. Allen's back and we shouldn't worry. We just need to keep an eye on him. Let Rhonda do her thing and take care of him. We've already seen positive results."

"Yeah, I guess you're right. I should be happy."

They spoke no more, quietly putting the rest of the groceries away. Sally paused and pulled her phone from her pocket.

"Dad, I think I'm going to go home, now. Tom and Eli will be there in a couple of hours, and I'd like to get some supper on for them. I'll call later and check on you."

"All right, Sally," he said, reaching to give her a hug. "Tell Eli, Pops loves him."

"I will, and if you end up going to Buck's place, don't stay too long."

Sy watched from the window, as Sally drove away. He considered his next move. Since Allen was feeling better and Rhonda was there to watch him, he'd go visit Buck. Not only would he get the shine he wanted, but Buck had something else too—, information. He always knew what was going on in town. Getting the scoop on that revival and the Sage character would be the first thing Sy would ask.

He told Allen and Rhonda he would be out for a while, then headed to his car.

Chapter Six

Small Town Odd

Driving through town, Sy saw new signs and posters everywhere announcing the tent revival. One large banner had even been strategically placed above the entrance of Sam's IGA sometime after he left the store that morning. The spectacle of the century, the gospel of the Sage. Come see the magic and experience a life changing event.

It seemed more like a carnival than a revival. The whole town was going crazy, a big love fest for this Sage and his party. Frowning, Sy shook his head and turned onto state route 1306. Driving for about a half mile, he made a left onto Hackworth Hollow, then continued uphill toward Buck's place.

Sy looked down onto the field below. He saw the Owen's farm with the tent, sides flapping in the wind, looking like a solemn stranger in the field. Like something from an old black and white horror film. The vampire waited inside, but no one knew until it was too late. Was the town in for a surprise? Was that Sage guy everything the town folk thought he was? Sy doubted it, but he seemed to be unsure of many things these days. A feeling of uneasiness crept into his bones, something cold. The shine he got from Buck would be welcome for the warmth alone.

The pavement ended, and he felt the car shimmy onto gravel. The passage had been neglected for a while, and Sy slowed the car to keep from bottoming out on the potholes. There were thick trees on both sides, and a large plume of dust arose in the air behind Sy's car as he continued uphill. The county road ended near a clearing, where an old single-wide mobile home trailer sat on an embankment.

The outer shell was white with rust streaks working from top to bottom. Several old tires adorned the roof to keep it from blowing away, something Buck would remove in the winter as the extra weight of snow could cause it to collapse. There were weeds and scrub trees surrounding the home. Junk cars and a few old lawnmowers posed as yard ornaments. A walkway of rocks, gathered from the nearby creek, led up to the front door.

To anyone else, the place would look long abandoned. But Buck preferred it that way. He didn't like visitors, except the ones who were coming to sample his brew.

Sy parked in a rough weeded driveway. Before he was fully out of the car, the door to the trailer flung open, and a scruffy bearded man peeked out. His old, frayed fishing hat read "TRUMP" in self adhered letters on the front. Producing a large smile, absent a few teeth, he welcomed his old friend.

"Sy! You old coon! What's you been up to?"

"Came to see if you had any brew. I got my son home and might need the medicine."

"For him or you?" Buck bellowed, followed by a raspy laugh.

"Probably both before it's done."

"Come on in. I got a fresh batch made up yesterday. Is that all you need? I had a pretty good crop this year too."

"You know me, Buck. I stick with the shine. Never was a smoker."

"You don't smoke this shit, it smokes you!" Buck laughed and slapped his knee. "Naw, I'm just a kiddin', I know you don't. If'n you come across anyone though, only if you can trust 'em, that is."

"Gotcha. I'll keep my ears open."

"How's old Allie doin'?" Buck said.

"He's better. Woke up earlier and the nurse is caring for him."

"Nurse? God damn! You got a woman at yer house? Is she a look-er?"

"Let's just say, I wouldn't throw her out of bed for eatin' crackers. She knows Allen, and I guess she knew Nicole, too. They were all friends when they lived in Lexington."

"Well, at least they got some history. Damn shame he fell into the hole. You seen that thing lately? It's gettin' bigger and comin' this way. It's only a mile over the hill there." Buck pointed a thumb toward the end of the trailer. "Hell, thing's going to swallow up the whole town. Wouldn't surprise me at all. You know the mine runs all under us. They's probably cracks everywhere."

"Yeah, Buck, I guess you're right. It'll probably get worse before it gets better. The sinkhole is a big one. I suppose we're lucky the fall didn't kill Allen. If he hadn't been so distraught over his wife dying, he wouldn't have fallen in at all. He's doing better, though. At least I got that."

"Yeah, you're right. Damn shame about Nicole. I remember her when she was a youngin', little curls bouncing on her head. She looked like a little angel with her blonde hair and blue eyes. I can still remember her and Allen playing together. You could tell they was somethin' special about those two. I knew her Daddy, too. Hell, he used to come over 'bout once a week to pass the jug. That was back when we was all workin' the mine. You two talk anymore?"

"Henry? No, we haven't talked much at all. Well, at least since they shut the whole mine operation down. I did see him at the funeral, but he didn't have much to say, probably still blames Allen for Nicole. Him and his boys aren't the easiest people to get along with, especially when they have a grudge to bear."

"I heard about all of that. You think they'd let that shit go. I couldn't see Allie doing anything to hurt Nicole. He was crazy about her; everybody could see it. Those two was always together. I think they left town to get away from Henry and his boys, Jesse more'n any of them. He's one crazy fucker!"

"Once they hear Allen's back in town, he'll have to deal with their bullshit. I'm not looking forward to it. Hey, Buck? Have you noticed anything weird goin' on around here? This tent and some guy named Sage?"

"Shit! I reckon. This whole place is goin' wild for him. It's like he's some country music singer or somethin'. He's makin' the old ladies and the young girls cream their jeans. He's like Elvis or somethin'."

"Where did he come from?"

"Hell if I know! He just rolled into town in his big Cadillac..."

"What did you say?" Sy interrupted. "A Cadillac?"

"Yeah, a big classic one. An old Fleetwood like the rich folk drive. I saw it out by the tent, along with a motor home."

"You're not going to believe this, but I think the same car followed me here. It was on the road when I left Lexington. When did you first notice it?"

"Yesterday morning, I think, and the Sage fella was in town the day before. He ain't the only one either. He's got some help. I went out there the other night." Buck's voice got higher, as he stood and pointed wildly in the direction of the tent. "They's a path in the woods out back, goes down to the Owen's place. I saw lights down there and thought maybe the DEA was onto me. They work with Sheriff Oeny, you know. I thought they was lookin' for my crop or even my still. So, I grabbed my shotgun and walked down the path, real quiet and all. Thank goodness the moon was full. I could see everything without needin' a flashlight. I saw the Cadillac there with two men unloading something. It looked like boxes. They was puttin' 'em all around the ground. They put a big sheet lookin' thing out, too. I'm guessing that was the tent. I reckon one of 'em was that Sage fella, all tall and good looking. But the other'n was a big fella. He was breathin' hard and suckin' on a plastic thing, one of them things kids use when they got the crup."

"An inhaler?"

Buck pointed at Sy. "Yeah, one of them. Well, all a sudden, they looked my direction. I hunkered down real quick. I don't think they saw me; they didn't come after me anyways. I sat there in the woods for a long time until they drove off. Funny thing is, they left all those boxes and the tent just sitting there on the ground. I waited a minute to make sure they wasn't comin' back. When I saw they wasn't, I turned around to leave, but before I did, I took one more look out in the field. It might have been the light playing tricks on my mind, or maybe what I was smokin', but I swear them boxes was a movin'."

"Moving? That's odd. What did you do?"

Buck shook his head., "I got the hell out of there, I did! Came back here and locked the doors. I don't ever lock my doors, but somethin' about all that didn't seem right to me."

"Watch yourself, Buck. I don't trust this guy. I think he's up to no good. Have you been back down there?"

"A couple of times, but they wasn't nobody around. I reckon the Sage fella is runnin' around town, drummin' up business. I ain't no religious man. I only go to church on Wednesday when they's passin' out free food. But I might go see what this revival is about. How about you?"

"I'm not sure yet. I'd advise you to think hard about it. Who knows what this guy is up to?"

"Well see, for me, it all depends if they's a givin' out free stuff or not." Buck grinned.

"Just be careful. Now, for what I came for."

Allen and Rhonda finished their third go at each other, and now lay panting, their naked bodies intertwined on the bed.

"Do you think your dad will notice we christened the place while he was gone?"

"I don't think he'll mind." Allen gave her a devious smirk.

Rhonda blew him a playful kiss. "What's there to do in this town anyway?"

"Well, not much. We could go for coffee at the new shop downtown, where the old diner used to be. I think it's called the Mountain Perk. I went there when I was in for the funeral. One thing I remember anyway."

"Sounds wonderful. We'll get hopped up on caffeine, and I can fuck your brains out some more."

"It's settled then. I suppose we should get dressed."

"Aww, do we have to?"

Allen smiled and bent to retrieve his underwear. He jumped from the playful slap Rhonda gave his bottom. She retrieved her clothes as well, and they both finished dressing. Once in the living room, Allen started to open the front door, then paused and looked at Rhonda.

"If I remember correctly, the coffee shop is across town, at least three miles away, and Dad's gone. Do you have a car?"

"Funny you should ask. It's pulling up right now." She nodded toward the door.

Allen regarded her questioningly before opening the window blind over the front door. He couldn't believe his eyes. A large black Cadillac, one like you'd see the president in, was parked outside.

Stepping ahead of Allen, Rhonda reached for the front door and opened it. "Our chariot awaits, my love."

Allen felt a twinge of royalty when a large man opened the back door of the car for him and Rhonda. He motioned for them to enter. The man's breathing was heavy, as if each breath was a labor to him. After Allen and Rhonda were seated, the man hesitated before closing the door. Allen watched him from the window, as he reached into his pocket, retrieving an inhaler. He placed it in his mouth then pushed the plunger and sucked inward. He took two puffs, the inhaler making a popping noise as he released it from his mouth. He lumbered forward and returned to the driver's seat.

"Who's he?" Allen said.

"His name is Samson, and he's a friend of mine from way back."

"He looks like a good guy to know." Allen noted the massiveness of the man. "Driver and protection, all rolled into one."

"Yes. Samson is the best."

"Where to, Rhonda?"

"To the coffee shop, Samson. Uh...the..."

"Mountain Perk," Allen finished for her.

"Yes, that one."

"No problem, we'll be there in one minute."

"I wasn't expecting limo services, Rhonda. You're full of surprises, aren't you?"

"Just wait, baby, you ain't seen nothing."

The Cadillac pulled off the highway toward the Mountain Perk. The near-empty parking lot made it easy for the large vehicle to maneuver through.

When Rhonda and Allen entered the cafe, the aroma of strong coffee wafted toward them. The Mountain Perk was only about three-quarters full, with a few patrons seated at tables and the rest at the counter, young kids taking advantage of the free wi-fi while busily tapping on their laptops and phones.

The decor was artsy with pottery from local artisans along the walls and on shelves that matched the dark wood laminate floors. Small round tables littered the right side of the shop, and a long bar with a glass cooler on one end adorned the other. Large espresso machines and coffee makers steamed behind the bar. It looked out of place in the small town, a welcome oasis of modernism in an area stuck fifty years in the past.

Two teenagers, a girl and a boy, worked behind the counter, busy brewing coffee and serving patrons. The girl had a shabby cut of hair colored a bright blue with piercings in her nose and gaged earlobes. Her name tag read "Nancy". The boy was tall with cropped red hair, his natural color, and tattoos adorning most of both arms. Both ears sported gauges, closed with skulls painted in the middle. He looked their way for a moment, then returned to work.

Rhonda and Allen regarded the large chalkboard menu on the wall, the daily specials jotted down in various colors. The girl stepped up to the counter.

"What can I get you?"

"I'll have a large latte and an almond biscotti. How about you Allen?"

"A large coffee, black, the dark roast."

"Okay, they'll be ready in a minute. It'll be ten dollars."

Rhonda paid the girl, and she and Allen made their way to the waiting area at the end of the bar. Once they received their order, they found a table to sit. Rhonda sipped her latte, blowing gently to cool it. Allen only considered his cup of coffee.

"What's wrong, baby?" Rhonda said.

"I don't know. I feel much better physically, but why can't I remember anything? I know you from before I was in the hospital, but I can't remember much else before waking up at Dad's. The strange thing is, I didn't even care until now. It's like my memories are starting to come back, but nothing is where it's supposed to be."

"Do you remember anything about, Nicole?"

"She was my wife at one time, and she died." He looked from Rhonda to the floor and furrowed his brow. "If she was my wife, I should remember her, right? What's happening to me?"

"Nothing, baby. You've gone through some trauma is all. I'm sure it's nothing, Allen. You remember me and all we had. That's progress."

"Well, not all we had. When did we become lovers?"

"Oh, baby, you don't remember. We had some things going on, but Nicole was cool with it."

"That's good. Maybe I need to talk to Dad. Does he remember what happened?"

"I don't know. But before you talk to him, I'd like for you to meet someone else."

"Who?" Allen said.

"On our way here, did you see the posters up everywhere around town?"

"For the tent revival?"

"Yes, those. The man on the pictures, the Sage. He's an old friend of mine. I'd like for you to see him. He's a hypnotist, you know?"

"A hypnotist? Why do you think I need to see a hypnotist?"

"He could help you to get some of your memories back. He's a great guy, really."

"I don't know. Maybe I should see Dad first, talk to him about all this."

"We will. But I'd like you to see the Sage. Do it for me?" Rhonda massaged Allen's arm and kissed his neck. She made her way up to his ear, blowing gently into it. "I'll make it worth your while."

Allen responded by giving her a deep kiss, which prompted two older ladies at the next table to smirk and mumble disapprovingly. Allen and Rhonda giggled before turning their heads to the sound of a bellowing voice nearby.

"Allen Sutton! When did you get back to town? I can't believe you have the balls to show your face around here." A young man about Allen's age got up and walked over to their table. The patrons close to Allen and Rhonda moved to the side of the shop, giving him a wide berth.

"I'm sorry. Do I know you?"

"Don't play dumb with me, Allen. If my brother hears you're back, he won't be happy. You should have stayed in Lexington."

Rhonda cocked her head sideways, looking at Allen. "Do you know this guy?"

"He should know me. I'm his brother-in-law, or I was anyway, until he killed my sister."

"You're Nicole's brother?"

"That's right. I'm Nathan, but I don't know why it's any of your business? Who are you? Did you know my sister?"

"Nathan? Is there a problem?" Nancy said from behind the counter.

Nathan looked at her with irritation. "No problem at all. Just having a friendly conversation."

"Okay, but don't forget, you're on the schedule during the concert. I want to go see the Sage, like everybody else."

"Sure, I told you to put me in place of you, so you can go. I don't care about no damned magician."

Nancy smiled and went back to work while Nathan turned his attention to Allen and Rhonda.

"My name is Rhonda Lane. I was friends with Nicole and Allen."

"You two look pretty chummy. You sure forgot about Nicole fast, didn't you, prick?"

Standing from the table, Allen stepped toward Nathan, hands raised in a peaceful gesture. "Listen, I don't know who you are, but cut me some slack. I just came out of a coma, and I'm having trouble remembering anything right now."

"Don't play me for a fool. I know you fell into that hole, but you look fine to me now. Why don't we talk outside before my brother gets here to have a word with you?"

Nathan pushed Allen on the shoulder, nudging him toward the entrance. Suddenly, Rhonda stood and jumped between them. She shoved Nathan, causing him to lose his balance. He stumbled clumsily and fell onto his bottom.

Nathan looked up at her, confused by the insult, and quickly jumped to his feet. Angrily, he drew back his hand to smack her, but she met his advance with a kick to the groin. The force of the blow caused Nathan to crumple to his knees as he grabbed his man parts, gasping for breath. People nearby jumped up from their tables, giving Nathan room to roll on the floor. Nancy and the boy barista came to check on him.

"C'mon, Allen. Let's get out of here."

Rhonda grabbed his arm, and Allen followed her. They made a hasty exit toward the door. Outside, the Cadillac was waiting for them.

"I think we may see him again. He'll probably have his brother with him the next time."

"Rhonda? How well did you know Nicole anyway?"

"Not particularly well. I used to hang out with the two of you when we all ran around Lexington."

"Were we a good couple?"

"I guess. You had your share of problems like most couples do, but you seemed fine to me. Don't worry, baby. The Sage will fix everything."

Chapter Seven

The Sage

It was early afternoon when Sy pulled into his driveway. Putting the car in park, he reached under the dash and pulled on the trunk release lever. The tail end of the car sprung open, and he stepped around to pull out two boxes with the words "Fresh Fruit" printed on the sides. Juggling one in his arms, he carried it up the steps of the porch. The quart jars clinked together as he walked. Sitting the box down, he returned for the other. He placed both boxes by the front door and stepped inside.

"Allen? Rhonda? You all want to give me some help here?"

He received no answer.

The bed in the spare bedroom was unmade. Sheets and bed and clothes were strewn on the floor. He supposed the kids were out on the town. *Did they walk?*

Shaking his head, he retrieved the boxes from the porch and placed them on the countertop. Sy reached for one of the jars. and pulled a glass from the cabinet, filling it a quarter of the way full. He took a sip and closed his eyes, relishing the feeling of the warm liquid coating his throat.

Carrying his glass with him, he went back to the spare bedroom to clean up a little. It looked like there'd been a wrestling match in the bed. He guessed Allen and Rhonda were becoming better acquainted and wondered just how well they knew each other before. After straightening the bed, he grabbed an empty clothes basket and began picking up the discarded clothes. A pair of lacy panties with a string where the ass end should have been rested under Allen's shirt.

Must be what they call a thong. He wondered why a girl would wear those things. Might as well not put anything on, instead of having your underwear riding up your crack. Seemed like it would be uncomfortable. He was sure to get a few looks at the laundromat with that stuff.

Sy placed the dirty clothes hamper in the corner for later and decided to retire to his easy chair for a nap. The glass was empty, and he didn't see the need to fill it again. As the saying went, a little goes a long way.

Allen and Rhonda cruised along Main Street in the back of the Cadillac. The roads would soon be busy with the people who worked out of town, returning for the day, but at that moment, they were empty. The townspeople stared as the Cadillac passed, and Rhonda, looking through the dark tinted window, flipped them off.

"What are you doing? They'll see you."

"Are you kidding me, Allen? How they going to see through those windows? Besides, the whole town will be in for an awakening they know nothing about soon enough. When Sage has the big concert on Friday."

"Yeah, about the Sage. Where exactly is he living?"

"In a motor home out by the tent. It's not his usual place, just where he lives while on the road. Don't worry, he's waiting for us. He has something to show you."

"Show me? He doesn't even know me," Allen said indignantly.

"He knows about you. I've told him. You'll see. We're almost there."

Rhonda squirmed with nervous anticipation. Allen, however, remained skeptical.

Where'd this guy come from, and how does Rhonda know him so well? Strange how she just mentioned him.

Allen realized he knew very little about her past. Rhonda had a familiarity to him, but that was all. He only had sparse memories of her but felt he could trust her.

The Owen's farm looked so familiar to him. Times playing in this field with his sister, maybe? His memories were fleeting. Everything before waking that morning was blurry. His dad and sister he remembered, but he had no memories of their past, only knew they were who they were. Nicole was in there, too, but only her presence. He couldn't even remember what she looked like. He knew she died but didn't know how, only remembered leaving the cemetery as they lowered the closed casket into the grave, then falling into a black abyss. The whole thing was strange and a bit frightening.

A strong breeze invaded the field as Allen stepped out of the car. It picked up dust and sent it in a small tornado along the road leading to the tent. The ominous structure stood tall in defiance. It seemed to have no affiliation with anyone, was its own entity, offering sanctity to sinners and the holy alike as the sides flopped aimlessly in the breeze. To the side of the tent sat a newer motor home.

Samson, moving fast for a man of his girth, led the way. But as they approached, Allen began to have doubts, a nervous suspicion things weren't right. He grabbed Rhonda's arm and turned her to face him.

"How do you know this guy?"

Pulling from his grasp, she sighed. "Why are you so tense, babe? I told you everything would be fine."

"I know, and I believe you. It's just, these memories keep flooding my head. They're muddled. You, Nicole, my family, all in there but no context of how and why. I can't seem to make a connection with anything."

"This is why you need to see the Sage. He's a healer and a magician. He can help. Trust me."

"Okay. Maybe you're right. I'm probably being nervous for nothing. It would be good to get things straight."

"Exactly. Now c'mon." She gave his hand a reassuring squeeze.

Samson held the door to the camper open and motioned them inside. The place was small but roomy enough with a couch and dinette melded together on one side and a kitchen on the other. A door separated the living area from the back of the camper. To the front, there were two small recliner chairs dividing the cab of the vehicle from the rest of the motor home. An opening lay between the chairs.

"Allen Sutton." A man appeared from the back of the RV. He was tall and thin, with a chiseled jaw and dark complexion. His hair was black and slicked back, eyes so blue they were like oceans. Dressed in a black tuxedo, the kind a magician would wear, his tie was loose, and the top of his shirt unbuttoned.

"Yes, and you must be Sage."

"You're correct, my friend. Rhonda has told me about you. You had a recent stay in the hospital, right?"

"That's right. Seems like everyone knows about me, but I know nothing of them. My memory is shot."

Sage gave a reassuring smile. "Yes, you took quite the fall. I'm sure there was some head trauma involved. Probably why you're having trouble remembering things. But the brain is a marvelous instrument and can heal if given the opportunity. Opening up certain avenues can help speed the process. I'm sure Rhonda has told you I'm a hypnotist?"

"She has. I'm not sure how it will help, but the stress of not being able to remember is too great. I'm willing to try anything at this point."

"Good. Sit, please."

Sage directed him to one of the recliner chairs. Allen watched as he opened the cover of a metronome sitting on the table, taking the arm all the way to one side before sending the device into motion. The soothing ticking sound it made had a calming effect, and Allen felt at ease.

"Are you comfortable?" Sage said.

"Yes, as well as I can be, I suppose."

"Good. Try to free your body of any tension."

Allen looked at Samson standing with Rhonda. The big man's nervous energy, even as he stood still, made it impossible to feel completely relaxed.

Sage noticed the distraction. "Samson? I feel you may be making our young friend a bit apprehensive. Could you wait outside please?"

Samson said nothing, only turned and left through the front door, the metal steps creaking as he descended.

"Am I okay to stay?" Rhonda asked.

Allen nodded. "You're fine."

Sage looked at Allen. "Okay then, continue to relax."

Allen did as he was asked and soon felt a haze of tiredness fill his body, a relaxed feeling, like before a much- needed nap. The metronome's rhythmic till consumed his thoughts.

"Now, listen to me and only me. I'm sending you to another place away from here, somewhere reality doesn't exist. The plane of your subconscious. You are like a bird, flying into the atmosphere, away from what you know. You will only come back to me when I say so. I'll count to ten and snap my fingers, then you will wake, but only when I say. Are we clear?"

"Yes."

"Good. Listen to the ticking and drift to sleep."

Waves of white filled Allen's eyesight and he felt lighter, his body seeming to lift away, like the bird Sage talked about, until he was floating over what appeared to be clouds.

After Allen was asleep, Rhonda pecked Sage on the shoulder. "Is he out?"

"He is. I'll begin to speak to him in a moment, once he sinks deep enough into his subconscious. When I do, our minds will connect."

"You'll be in his mind? Wow, I didn't think hypnotism worked that way."

"It doesn't. My powers are greater than your typical hypnotist. You know how we work. The power of our creator binds us all and gives abilities from the energy of the collective. It's also what keeps us eternally young. Does he know about Rebecca yet?"

"No, I didn't want to take a chance losing him, but I have the meeting planned as soon as you plant the seed in his brain. You can charm him enough for me to get him to the mine, right? I'm afraid if I took him there now, he'd freak once he saw the sink hole."

"You can be assured, Rhonda, he'll be a very willing participant once his mind is at ease. I want him to accept Rebecca as much as you do. She's counting on it."

"I know. She has to have one from the soil he or she grew up on, so she can re-corporate. I can understand why she wants him. He's the most pure person I've ever known." Rhonda smiled thoughtfully. "Well, he was until I got hold of him. Once his wife was out of the way, he was all mine."

"But he had to fall in a sinkhole and lose his memory first. I'm not so sure you did your job as well as you could have."

Rhonda frowned at Sage's insinuation. "My powers of desire and persuasion work extremely well. I didn't know his wife was pregnant. When he found out, all my plans started to unravel. I had to do something to get him to Rebecca. Although I don't fully understand why she needs him. I always thought the mixed body parts were her power source."

"Rebecca's ways are infinite. We'll never completely understand them."

"Well, whatever. Use your power of charm to get Rebecca what she wants." She looked at Allen, calmly sleeping. "He'll make a welcome addition to the general class. Once you're in there, make sure he's good and ready to meet her."

"Don't worry, I will." Sage turned to Allen and placed himself directly in front of the sleeping man's face. "Can you hear me, Allen?"

"Yes, I hear you."

"Good, let's come down now to the room below you. I'll be there."

Allen pointed his feet down and descended from the clouds to land in a room very familiar to him. Sage stood there but only a form of him, hazy and fuzzy like poor television reception. Yet his voice was as clear as if he were standing right next to him.

"Where are we?" Allen asked.

"We're in your house, the one you lived in while in Lexington."

Allen stood in a room with a high ceiling. Several windows adorned the walls, allowing light to pour in. He could hear birds chirping outside, a spring day with all the promise of new life, shucking the cold of winter's death. Allen saw an opening leading to a staircase and heard a voice calling from upstairs.

"Allen, can you come up here? I need help."

He looked to Sage for guidance. "Is that Nicole?"

"Go to her and find out."

Allen walked to the bottom of the stairs and hesitated a moment, then ascended the steps to the upper floor. At the top, there was a hallway with four doors—two on the left side, one to the right, and the last at the very end. Only the door on the right was open.

"Allen? Where are you? I need you," a woman's voice called.

He saw her there, naked, her body voluptuous and inviting. She looked exotic, with dark hair and skin, eyes as black as onyx, deep with no other color. She looked almost alien, but he felt no inhibitions over her appearance, only warmth inside.

"Nicole? Is it really you?"

"Yes, Allen, don't be silly. Come here. I've been waiting for you to come home."

He realized for the first time he was naked also and eased over to her. His arms wrapped around her waist, pulling her into him. His erection met with her midsection, feeling the warmth. She kissed him, deep and erotic, causing him to become even more aroused, before separating from him. She grabbed his wrist and guided him to a bed in the middle of the room. Her body stretched across the mattress, and she rolled onto her back, spreading her legs, and coaxing him toward her.

Allen eased into her, rhythmically moving up and down. He was sure he'd been there many times; the familiarity was overwhelming.

Sage smiled from the doorway, pleased with the way he had guided his muse to Rebecca. He supposed it was time to bring his young friend back to reality but decided to wait a bit. *Allow the boy to have some fun.*

He turned for the stairwell, figuring he would give the couple a little privacy, but was stopped by the sight of a picture on the wall.

Someone he was sure he recognized, a girl from long before.

The photo was black and white, a sepia- colored antique like the ones he remembered from his youth. *How long ago? Over a hundred years?* Time passed so fast that he could barely recall. He shook his head and relaxed, preparing to wake and give the sequence to bring Allen back. But instead of clearing his head, he was overwhelmed by a woman's voice, one he strangely recognized.

"Damien? Damien, are you there?"

He turned toward the invader and saw a ghost, the kind he'd seen before, black and white, flickering like an old movie in the peculiar way they did. They always walked when the parts began to stir, but in all the years he'd seen them, one never spoke to him. The name she called him had not been one he was used to hearing, not since he was young, fresh from the war, his wife dead from childbirth and his daughter gone, sent away to live with his brother and her wife. But it was her, he was sure of it.

"Sarah? How? You can't be here. You're dead."

"Not Sarah, Damien, but her granddaughter, Sadie. The child of the daughter you left behind to join this group. Why so surprised? I'm dead, and you know the dead walk when the parts return."

"Yes, but they don't speak. This is all wrong. Leave me; let me wake."

"No, Damien, I'm here to warn you. There is a disturbance in the spirit world. Rebecca must go, and you have a decision to make. Stay with her or die. Don't try to take him." She pointed toward the bedroom. "He's mine."

He closed his eyes and tried to ignore her, then heard Rebecca scream.

"Sage! I'm losing him. What are you doing?"

He opened his eyes but saw no ghost; Sadie was gone. Sage ran to Rebecca. Blood dripped from the walls and pooled on the floor of the bedroom. Rebecca held the limp body of Allen, half on and half off the bed. She was struggling, as if he were being pulled into the blood gathering on the floor.

Another figure stood nearby, a young girl with an opening in her head where one of her eyes should have been. It was large and gaping, burnt black on the perimeter. Sage had seen that kind of wound in the war. It was clearly made by a gun. Blood poured in fountains from the area, covering the floor around the bed.

In odd contrast to the wound was the other side of her head. It was intact, and Sage could see stringy blonde hair and a wide blue eye staring at him, confused.

"What is this? Who is this girl?" Rebecca asked.

"I'm not sure. Maybe a memory he's retaining."

"Sage! Wake him, now, before he sees this."

Trying to focus, trembling with goose-bumped flesh, Sage looked at his arm. *How is this possible? I'm not supposed to be physical here.*

"What's wrong? You seem distracted."

"Nothing, my queen. I'll wake him now."

He took a deep breath and released it, willing himself awake. Rhonda and Samson were pacing about the room. They turned to him.

"What happened? Allen was moving all over the place. He looked like he was in pain or something," Rhonda said.

"I don't know. Something in his mind, an old memory I guess, distracted me."

"Is everything ready? Can I take him to see her?"

Visibly shaken, Sage sat beside Allen and began to count backward from ten. When he reached one, he snapped his fingers and Allen stirred, then woke.

"Allen? Are you okay?" Rhonda said.

"Huh? I guess. What happened? I was with Nicole, then everything got fuzzy. I did see her though. I at least know what she looks like."

"Well, don't struggle too hard, because we're going to meet someone to help you with all your troubles." She looked at Sage. "I suppose I should have taken him there first. He's no better now than he was before."

"Don't patronize me. I've done this hundreds of times and never had a negative result."

Allen was trying to focus on the conversation. "Is everything okay? Am I causing you all trouble?"

"No, you're fine, babe. Let's get out of here."

Allen stood, wobbled for a minute, and followed her toward the door. Samson walked behind them.

Sage tried to gather his thoughts, to meditate for a moment and pull himself together. But as he stood, he saw a wisping figure floating near the back of the motor home. It was her, his granddaughter. She smiled at him as he walked toward her but faded before he got too close.

He couldn't understand what was happening. The dead had always been present when the parts came back, but they had never been coherent in any form. They only hovered in the background. A presence. One to ignore. But that ghost knew things about him no others knew save Rebecca and Samson.

His real name hadn't been spoken in years. He'd almost forgotten it, but now with it weighing heavy in his head, he couldn't help but remember. He was once Damien Reynolds, a returning soldier from World War One. Rebecca had never seemed to worry about them either, but he wondered if they were talking to her as well.

These were all things to worry about, but not now, there was too much work to do. He had a revival to get ready for, and the people needed a Sage, not a Damien. He opened the door and stepped out to catch up with Samson. It was time to release the parts and bring the tent alive.

Buck Stanley had a curious nature, always poking his nose where it didn't belong. In fact, his daddy used to tell him to stay out of everybody's business. He remembered sneaking to the barn as a child, where his daddy and some other men were talking. He knew the barn was off limits to him, especially when Daddy had guests in there, but the men had pulled up on motorcycles, and Buck, hearing the roar of Harley engines invading the night, felt compelled to see what was going on. He snuck out of the house and crawled up a ladder behind the barn, then eased into the loft without being detected.

The men had long hair and sleeveless motorcycle jackets with letters on the back. Their arms were covered in tattoos. Buck got excited because he saw a naked lady drawn on one of them. His daddy was handing them sandwich bags full of green, dried leaves. Buck had seen these before in Daddy and Mamma's bedroom, another place off limits to him. After they put the bags away, they handed Daddy more cash than Buck had ever seen. They walked out of the barn.

Buck heard the motorcycles fire up and waited until the noise faded, then climbed down from the loft. When he reached the bottom rung of the ladder, he noticed his daddy standing there. He received the whipping of his life for disobeying orders.

"This is dangerous stuff I do, and you can't ever let your guard down," his daddy said. "I know I'm hard on you. But you need to be tough. Don't trust anybody you don't know."

So, from then on, Buck made it his business to know his neighbors and only trust the families and people he knew. Sy was a friend from when he worked the mines. Henry's boys were pretty good, too. They could distribute his goods around to their friends.

Buck's daddy supplemented his income with the drug and alcohol trade, but he never had the knack for staying clear of the law the way Buck did. He always made the same mistake; he didn't follow his own advice and sold to the wrong people. The fed's arrested Daddy a few days after he met with the motorcycle men in the barn. Old Sheriff Oeny, Ralph Oeny's daddy, was with them. Buck still remembered what the old sheriff said.

"Looks like you bought it this time, Ray. We got you dead to rights. You really fucked up." The sheriff laughed as he put Buck's daddy in the patrol car, another reason Buck hated the sheriff so much. They drove off with Buck and his momma looking on from the front porch.

"Serves the piece of shit right. He never treated us decent, took all that money and spent it on his whores," Momma said.

Soon after, they lost their farm. Momma sold it cheap once she found it was near foreclosure. Daddy ended up in the penitentiary, facing twenty-five to life, and Momma, with nothing better to do, left with a man she had been seeing. Buck went to live with his grandpa, who was meaner than shit and didn't want anything to do with him. So, he ended up in foster care. By then, he was sixteen and nobody wanted him. He bounced around the system until he was eighteen. Then the damnedest thing happened. His grandpa wanted him to come care for him.

"I'm old and near death from the COPD. You help me, boy, and I'll give you my place here. They's near twenty acre and this trailer. It ain't much, but it's better than nothin'. Ray is still rotting in jail, the worthless prick he is. If'n he ever gets out of prison, don't let him come back and take this. It'll be yours," his grandpa said, coughing.

Buck agreed, and when his grandpa died and his work in the Salt mine dried up, he turned to the only other business he knew. Grandpa needn't have worried about his daddy coming back to take the farm though, because he never came up for parole. Apparently, those bikers were murdered nearby, and since he had dealings with them, Buck's daddy was implemented in their deaths. Now his daddy was seventy-one years old. He figured the man would die in prison before he got out. Buck would visit him occasionally and always got an earful.

"Watch yerself, Buck. They's some crazy shit going on in that town. Don't trust anybody. Those bikers were found in the mine. They tried to say I did it, because I was the last one they was seen with. But I swear I didn't. Something drug them in there. I don't know what, but something. I always heard strange shit went on in there."

Buck remembered stories of missing people in the mines, but he figured they got lost or fell in one of the bottomless pits marked off limits. But his daddy seemed to be talking about something else entirely.

"They was found mutilated, their body parts strewn all over the place. I'm not capable of somethin' like that. The only reason they pinned it on me is because of those parts they found. But they vanished. Somebody came into county and stole 'em. They thought I did it. They're going to keep me here forever, though, no matter what I say. But I swear, I didn't do it. Somebody else took 'em. Don't trust anybody around there, I tell ya!"

Daddy told him that story a few months ago, then he was transferred to a federal prison up north. The whole thing had him spooked, and now somebody was putting up a tent right next door to him? It all seemed a little too strange.

Maybe I should investigate the situation, before they come over here on my property.

Buck waited until dark, long after Sy Sutton left with his goods. He put his mud boots on, pulling them tight against his feet. Then snugged his treasured MAGA cap—signed at a rally by the man himself—tight against his head. He reached for his shine, took a few swigs, and toked from the blunt he'd just rolled to get his courage up. Sufficiently relaxed, he grabbed his shotgun and tucked a flashlight in the pocket of his overalls. The July air was humid but breezy, making it pleasant for hiking.

Clouds covered the moon, hindering his visibility. So he turned on the flashlight, making sure to point it down so nobody in the distance could see. Buck was halfway to the tent when he spotted the large canvas structure, whipping blissfully in the night wind. He turned off the flashlight and eased into the field from the edge of the woods. Buck crept toward a tree, hiding behind its trunk, a maneuver he'd performed many times when hunting an elusive deer.

The tent stood almost close enough to touch. There was a motor home parked beside it along with the Cadillac. Buck started to step into the clearing but was startled by voices and ducked back behind the tree. Four people walked toward the tent.

Buck only recognized one of them. It was Allen Sutton, Sy's boy. *He looks pretty good for someone who just got out of the hospital.* He wondered if the girl with him was his nurse. *Sy's right, she is a looker.* The other two were people he didn't know at all. One was tall and skinny and the other a big fella who looked scary. They all disappeared into the tent.

Once they were gone, Buck studied the structure. The large canvas was similar to an old circus tent with wooden poles poking from the top, supporting the edges and center. There were two flaps of heavy fabric hanging over the entranceway to serve as doors. A slight breeze blew back one of the flaps, and Buck could see what he perceived as movement inside. *Probably the bunch who just went in.* It was hard to tell from where he stood.

He pushed the shotgun tight into his shoulder and rested the barrel on his forearm. Buck eased into the clearing, wanting to get a closer look. Carefully making his way toward the tent, he saw a light flickering from somewhere in the middle of the enclosure. The light was weak, the kind produced from a lantern or coal oil lamp. No one was moving around. *If Allen's in there, he might be in trouble. Weren't all these people strangers?*

"Fuck it," he murmured.

He raised the shotgun to level and walked through the entrance of the tent. Once inside, Buck looked around. The place was much larger than it appeared from the outside, and he couldn't see the ceiling, only a dark abyss that seemed to go on forever. There was a stage toward the back, but Allen was nowhere to be seen, nor any of the other people who'd gone in with him. In the middle of the room, there was a small fire with a strange, blue-colored flame, like propane, partially illuminating the air above it. As he stepped closer to it, Buck's eyes widened.

Things weaved in and out from the darkness to the light of the flame. The movements reminded him of moths, but those things weren't insects. They were body parts. Arms, legs, and even heads, all suspended and spinning in the air. One arm had a tattoo that looked like a naked lady he remembered from long ago.

"What the fuck?" he said aloud.

A spinning head stopped and considered him for a moment, then gave a crazed laugh, unnerving Buck. Instinctively, he fired the gun but missed the head, or anything else. The blast of the gun muted in the darkness above. An arm fell from the air and hovered in front of him, giving him a one finger salute. Buck had seen enough.

Holding the shotgun in front of him, the barrel shaking furiously, he fired again, the shot harmlessly disappearing into nothingness. With eyes wide and his breath quickening, he walked backward toward the entrance to the tent. He turned on his heels to run but stopped, confronted by the large, scary man. Buck guessed him to be at least six-foot-eight and three hundred pounds. The other man was standing beside him, wearing a tuxedo and a top hat like a magician. The large man took a puff from an inhaler, making a popping sound as he pulled it from his mouth. He breathed deep, then exhaled.

"Hello," the tuxedo man said.

Buck pulled the shotgun tightly into his shoulder and leveled it at the man's head.

"I know who you are. You's that Sage fella been going all over town," Buck said.

The tall man stepped back and bowed, removing his hat as he did. "Yes, I'm the Sage, and this is my establishment." He waved his hand in a large circular motion.

"I don't care what you are. I don't like the shit you're pulling over here! You stay the fuck away from me."

Sage put his hand on the gun barrel, pushing it away. "There's no need for violence, we're all friends here."

"Ain't nobody touches my gun, motherfucker!" Buck pulled the trigger, wincing as he did, but nothing happened. His finger was frozen in place.

"Put the gun down, Buck," Sage said.

Staring at Sage in disbelief and feeling strangely like he had no other choice; Buck lowered the gun.

"H-how did you know my name?"

"I know lots of things. Now come with me, I have something to show you."

Buck followed Sage to the middle of the tent where the body parts flew in circles around his head. Dismembered arms clawed and grabbed his skin. The teeth in the mouths of the heads chattered, like someone who was freezing in the cold.

"Behold, these are my bodies, broken for you. Let them eat of your flesh and you will be one with us!" Sage raised his arms in the air and stepped from the circle, allowing the parts to descend upon his guest.

The parts covered him from head to toe, and he screamed from sheer terror. Buck fell to his knees as his body was bitten and torn into. He felt as though he was being pulled in different directions, his flesh tearing, blood leaving his body and pooling onto the ground. They swarmed him, efficient in their death blows, buzzing in the air as though a hive of angry bees. His body jerked from one side then to the other until no pain was felt, only pleasure.

Curiosity had finally beaten Buck. His daddy always told him it would. But strangely, instead of feeling fear for his death, he'd never felt more alive.

CHAPTER EIGHT

UNLIKELY FRIENDS

When Sy woke from his nap, it was dark outside. The short sleep he intended had turned into a siesta. He rubbed his eyes and stretched, sitting upright in the recliner chair. Lights from a car pulling into the driveway illuminated the wall in front of him. He figured it was Allen and Rhonda returning.

He looked out the window and saw Aa Toyota Corolla parked in his drive with only one occupant inside, a female by the look of it. She stepped out of the car, but in the dim light, he couldn't make out who it was. She was almost to the door when Sy opened it. To his surprise, he saw someone he thought he'd never see again.

"Patty? What are you doing here?"

"If I could come in, I'll explain," she said.

"I guess." Sy reluctantly pulled the door wide.

She looked different than the last time he saw her. For starters, she was more casually dressed than in the hospital. The sensible polo shirt and khakis were replaced by ripped denim jeans and a t-shirt. Her hair was down, not up in the tight ponytail she wore before. Overall, she seemed more relaxed, not the iron lady she had been. Sy welcomed the change but wouldn't let his guard down so quickly.

"How's Allen? Is he doing okay? I've been worried since the other night."

"He's good. I was actually expecting him and Rhonda when you pulled up."

"Rhonda? Rhonda Lane? What's she doing here?"

"She's Allen's nurse. We—my daughter and I that is—have hired her to stay with Allen and take care of him."

"How's that working out?"

"So far so good. He's responding well to the treatment she gave him. He's already out and about, feeling much better."

"He's up? Walking on his own?"

"Yes. Like I told you, I was expecting him and Rhonda when you arrived."

"I see. I find it strange he's had such a miraculous recovery. I was half expecting you to take him back to the hospital by now."

Sy smirked, realizing the old Patty may be surfacing. "You would've liked it if I did, I'm sure, but you don't need to worry. All he needed was to get away from that horrible place."

"No, don't get me wrong. I'm glad, too. I don't work for the hospital anymore. I was fired the next day, after the night you took Allen home. Not long after Harley escaped. He left the grounds, and nobody knows where he is."

Sy was surprised by this revelation and started to feel some remorse for her. "Wow, a lot happened since we left. Sounds like the whole place fell apart."

"Yes, it did. Look, Sy, I'm sorry we didn't get started on better terms. I can be a little rough around the edges sometimes. Probably why I got the job in the first place. I'm also sorry I didn't see what was going on with Allen. I could have handled the whole situation much better."

"I guess it all turned out the way it was supposed to. You could have sent the law or adult protective services against me, but you didn't. Since you're no longer a nurse there, I guess we're on a level playing field now. Can I get you something to drink? Coffee or anything?"

"Sure, do you have anything stronger than coffee though? It's been a rough few days. The wound on my shoulder is still throbbing."

"Yeah." Sy grinned. "I have something."

"Good, but only a little. I have to find a hotel later. By the way, where is the nearest one?"

Sy chuckled as he poured the moonshine into a small glass, then handed it to Patty. "Did you see any on the way in?"

"No. But it was getting dark. I did stop by a gas station. I asked the attendant behind the counter about the hotel and that I was looking for you. But all he gave me was directions to your house. Then he gave me a wink and smiled?"

"Probably Moe Spencer. He's always friendly with the ladies. He sent you here because we have no hotel in town."

"Well, he was rude, and he needn't try to come onto me. I'm not really into men. You surely figured that, didn't you?"

Sy shuffled nervously. "Oh, well, whatever you do in your personal life is your business. I may have assumed. Rhonda never mentioned it or anything."

Patty shook her head. "What has the little slut said about me?"

"Okay, you two may not be on the best of terms." Sy watched her take a gulp of moonshine. "But she's been nothing but a godsend to us. We needed a nurse and she stepped in."

She swallowed hard, not even wincing. *Buck's best brew didn't faze her?* Sy thought this girl was tough, but now he was sure of it.

"I suppose she's a good nurse, but I think it a bit strange how she left the hospital right after you did, before I could say anything to her, then shows up here and takes Allen out? How did she get him up? Did she use a wheelchair?"

"You don't understand. He was walking and talking on his own this morning, like nothing ever happened to him."

"How's that possible? It would take days, maybe weeks, to get the drugs out of his system, and then his muscles had atrophied, or gotten smaller. How would he even have the ability to move, let alone walk on legs? This doesn't make much sense."

"I suppose medical miracles are possible, aren't they? Maybe Allen is one?"

"I've seen some pretty miraculous things, Sy, but nothing like what you described. I'm concerned for your son's well-being."

"Don't worry, Patty, I'm sure he's in good hands."

"Really? You may want to think about it. You don't find it a little convenient she showed up so soon after you brought Allen back? I'm not sure what she was up to in the hospital, but it looks like she may have brought it here. Where is Rhonda anyway?"

"I haven't seen her or Allen since this morning. What do you mean, what she was up to?" Sy asked.

"When you took Allen...Well, the whole thing seemed a little fishy to me. I put the orderlies in front of the door to guard you and told the guards downstairs to be on the lookout. Were any of them where they were supposed to be? Didn't you think it was fairly easy to get out?"

"I wouldn't say easy, but it wasn't as hard as I thought it would be."

"I think she planned on you getting him out of there, and when you came through the door, she used it to her advantage."

"I don't see how it's possible for her to have set up Allen's escape up. Wouldn't she have just left with him when her shift was over?" Sy said.

"She couldn't without getting caught. She was waiting for the right moment, and then you came along. She wanted Allen out of there. But why?"

Sy shrugged. "She told me they were friends before he got to the hospital. She even said she worked with him occasionally."

"Yes, I remember Allen worked for the hospital. He was a social worker. Could I have another please?" Patty held the glass in front of her.

Sy decided to have a small one himself. He hadn't seen a woman drink that much, ever. He was quite impressed.

"Sy? I hate to be forward, but can I crash here tonight? Unless you know of another place I can stay."

"No, not at all. You may have to sleep on the couch when Allen gets back." He thought about Rhonda. *Where would she sleep?* His little place was getting more cramped. He'd have to think about the arrangements later, because the way Patty was drinking, she'd need a place to crash. At that rate, she'd be lucky to find her car the next day.

"Sy? Did Rhonda give Allen anything?"

"She ran an IV. She said it was saline and electrolytes."

"What? That's basically a sport drink. We would typically use that to help someone recover, but it wouldn't happen overnight."

"I don't know. Maybe there was more in there, something she didn't tell us about."

"Obviously. Where's the empty solution bag? I want to see what she gave him."

"My daughter threw it in the trash earlier. It may still be there. I'll check." Sy walked to the spare bathroom and retrieved the discarded bag, thankful the trash hadn't been emptied yet. He took it to Patty for inspection.

She frowned. "I've never seen anything like this. The manufacturer is someone I've never heard of either. The Pendleton Corporation?"

Sy stared at her. "What did you say? Who made it?"

"It's right here, on the bottom of the bag."

Sy saw the name in small red print, the same people he worked for, the ones who owned the mine. Strange they'd be making medical supplies, but they were a big company.

"I worked for them. They owned the mine. It shut down a few years ago, though. Not long before my wife died."

"That is strange. Maybe Rhonda was working for them as well?" Patty handed the bag back to him. "I didn't realize you were a widower."

"Yeah, Sadie's been gone for over a year now. It's been hard, but I manage to keep this old sack of bones going."

"Old? You're not old. You can't be much older than me."

He looked at her and smiled. "I'm fifty-five, actually."

"Well, I'm forty-five, so not much distance between us at all."

"I guess you're right, but since she's been gone, I feel like I've aged by thirty years."

"Then, maybe it's time to turn the clock back. I think sometimes we have to let go of the past to see how much more life we have to live. I left my girlfriend yesterday. Another reason why I'm here. Once I started moping around, I got to thinking about Allen and how much of a mess I'd made at the hospital and decided it was time to make amends. But now, I'm worried something may have happened to him, even if he is healthy. Don't you think we should find them?"

"I guess. It is getting late, and I figured they'd be here by now. I could take a look around town. You can wait here for me if you'd like."

"Who? Me? I'm going, too. Let me get my keys from my purse." Patty reached for it and missed entirely, nearly tumbling face-first onto the carpet.

"I think I should drive," Sy said.

"You may be right. Well, since I have a DD now, maybe I could bring one of those jars with me? I seem to be developing an affinity for the stuff."

Sy thought it strange to hear her laugh but found it did have an infectious quality. "It looks like it. Sure, but maybe only a quarter of one. A little goes a long way."

Patty stood and stumbled forward, catching herself before she fell. Sy couldn't remember the last time he babysat a drunk, especially one that attractive, but only shook his head. He poured some of the shine into a quart jar he retrieved from the cabinet and walked with Patty out the door.

In his wildest dreams, he would never have guessed he'd be going out on the town with the one and only Patty Hudson, and a drunk one at that. It was proving to be a night he'd never forget.

Once they left the tent, Rhonda and Allen walked along a path in the woods for a quarter of a mile until they came to a clearing. The area around it was devoid of grass or any other vegetation. The earth was cracked, splintering in many different directions but all diverging in one central location in the middle of the barren field. Rhonda, carrying a small flashlight, guided Allen like an expert who knew the area well to where the large hole gaped open, dark and foreboding.

Allen recognized the sink hole and hesitated. He tried to pull Rhonda away from it, his reservations getting the best of him. She coaxed him forward by massaging the front of his pants, smiling at the erection he produced.

Pointing the flashlight toward the sinkhole, Rhonda shined the beam onto the edge of the cavern. A rope ladder hung there, descending into the darkness. Guiding Allen to it, she let him go first and then followed close behind. Once they made it to the bottom, she shined the light into a tunnel. The air was cold and damp. Pieces of quartz shimmered along the ceiling, giving it a mystical feeling like they had gone back in time to some medieval dungeon. Allen wondered if they would come across a dragon. As they walked along, a smaller passageway became visible off the main tunnel.

"C'mon. This is where we're going."

Staring down the corridor, Allen asked, "Rhonda? What's in there?"

"Not what. But who." She grabbed his hand and smiled.

As they left the larger tunnel, he noticed wooden beams holding up the ceiling. Allen knew where they were—the mine where his dad worked for many years. But it looked like an older section, one he doubted his dad knew about. Rhonda clipped along, striding with purpose.

"Up ahead. Not too far now," she said.

At the end of the passageway, rocks piled up against the sides of the wall, and large wooden cross tie beams lay on the ground, splintered in two. An opening lay beyond. Rhonda shined the flashlight along the ground to help Allen see where he was going. They stepped into a large, round room. Red lights pulsed from within the walls, making the place look alive. As they walked farther into the room, the lights became brighter, so bright the flashlight was no longer needed.

The temperature in there was much warmer than the passageway. He noticed cracks, large ones, starting in the middle and getting smaller as they stretched out to the sides in what looked to be a pattern of some kind. The ground pulsed beneath him, and suddenly Allen felt anxious.

"Rhonda? What is this?"

"Life, Allen. It's the living, breathing essence of life. A power you can't imagine. But with me by your side, you'll be able to harness a portion of it."

"I don't get it."

"You will." Rhonda took her clothes off and prodded Allen to do the same. As he did, the warmth in the room intensified and Rhonda's heat with it as she rubbed her body against his, coaxing him to the middle of the room. She pointed to the ceiling. There was a hole, looking to be about ten feet in diameter.

"The tent is right above here, Allen. This place breathes it's life force into it."

Allen considered it for a moment but looked away, feeling a presence close to him. Standing by the wall of the room was a naked and shivering girl. She leaned against the rock, her hands pawing at the stone, as if she were nervous and couldn't relax. Blonde, stringy hair lay matted against her head, and her skin was gray, hanging loosely on her frame. She looked young but haggard, as if she'd lived a rough life.

Rhonda noticed Allen staring at something. "What are you looking at?"

"The girl over there. Don't you see her?"

Rhonda looked in the same direction but saw nothing. "There's no one there, babe," she said, stroking his midsection. "C'mon, lets walk over this way a bit."

Allen wasn't aroused anymore, only continued to stare at the girl as she turned to him. He could see the other side of her, or what was left of it. A black hole where her eye should be, was seeping brackish blood. Allen grimaced but felt strangely calm, as if he knew her, even felt sorry for her. He felt compelled to soothe her.

Rhonda pulled at his arm, urging him to come with her. "What are you doing? There's nothing there."

Allen pulled away from her and stepped toward the girl. He stopped. A baby, or half of one, the lower section missing, crawled from behind her, its small hands digging for purchase on her loose skin, stopping when it reached her breast. Its head prodded then attached to the nipple, sucking furiously for nourishment. The girl reached for Allen and smiled with black teeth, some missing, worms crawling through the vacant spaces. But he wasn't deterred, only felt a stronger connection to her. He touched her outstretched hand. His thoughts were invaded by warmth, something familiar, like a day he'd spent with his family years ago as a child. He followed the girl.

Rhonda reached for his hand, but before she could grab it, a figure appeared beside her, an older woman, maybe middle-aged. It was a ghost, like the ones she'd seen before, flickering in and out like an old reel type movie. Rhonda thought she vaguely resembled Allen. The woman placed her hand on Rhonda's wrist, and Rhonda regarded her strangely, never having been touched by one of the ghosts before. Her reservations turned to terror, though, as smoke formed in the air, and she felt her flesh burning.

"Rebecca! Help me," Rhonda cried out.

The ground shook, and a screech echoed throughout the chamber. Allen put his hands to his ears to protect them. The girl's image thinned then dissipated completely, as did the ghost. Confused, he pulled his hands from his head and turned to Rhonda, who was massaging her wrist.

"It's okay, Allen. Come with me. Rebecca will make it all better."

"Who?"

"Rebecca, the one who gives the power to us. I am one with her collective, and soon, you will be too. Some will be soldiers in her army, but others have been chosen to be generals. Aren't you happy to be among the chosen few?"

She led him to the center of the room. He jumped when he saw a large eye staring back at him from a hole in the ground. Allen felt a strange surge in his body as a force overcame him. Rhonda, smiling, began to glow red hot. Allen, feeling the urge to have her, pulled Rhonda close to him, absorbing her intense heat.

Tentacles formed from below them, wrapping around their legs and easing upward, stopping just below their midsections. Then, separating from the others, one tentacle hovered in the air momentarily and entered Rhonda's body through her womanhood. She gasped, throwing her head back.

Allen, aroused by the motion, worked his mouth up and down her neck before placing his lips to hers and kissing her deeply. He felt the tickling of a tentacle working its way into him. Power pulsed through him, making him feel more alive than he ever had.

He grinded his hips to Rhonda's middle, and she straddled him. He held her bottom and entered her, thrusting with her pulsations. As she pushed her chest into his face, she threw her head back again. Allen could feel the tentacle inside him, working its way around to find a home. It seemed as aroused as he was, quivering somewhere near the middle of his chest.

Suddenly, he felt the overwhelming need to taste Rhonda's flesh, so strong he couldn't let it go. The blood running through her arteries and veins called to him. He couldn't help himself, no matter how disgusting his mind tried to make it. He lusted for her sustenance, her life. His mouth quivered as he tried to will it to open.

Rhonda sensed his hesitation. "Eat my flesh, Allen. We need you to."

Her chest pulsed red hot, and Allen's reservations fell. He bit into it and chewed on the soft meat. Blood flowed down his chin and onto his body. Instead of blood falling to the floor, it rose into the air, creating a vortex around them.

The tentacles released them, allowing Allen and Rhonda to be levitated. Below them, a woman rose from the ground, her olive skin glowing lightly. Her raven dark hair flowed against it, falling loosely down to her waist. She wore no clothing, her features flawless and perfect, and she smiled at the spectacle above her.

Allen felt her presence in his mind, as the brilliance of thousands of worlds opened to him at once. Histories older than time itself rolled through his thoughts, overwhelming him. It was more than his mind could take, more than it was supposed to absorb, and his head began to ache from the insult. Then, as quickly as they'd come to him, the thoughts subsided and all he could see was her, Rebecca, in all her loving glory. Her voice calmed him, and he longed for it to be there.

Allen, be with me, always. Take her and eat. Taste my blood in her and be one with the hive.

He bit into Rhonda again and again, chewing on pieces of her flesh, consuming her, until she broke apart. Pieces of her body—arms, legs, her head—floated in the air, mixed with blood and bodily fluids, the suspended ooze of Rhonda's being.

Allen felt something deep within him wanting out. He regurgitated a massive amount of blood, spewing the contents of his stomach into the air and onto the body parts floating before him. A small balloon-like thing started to form, bloody and bulging, with veins protruding on the outside. It began to expand and grow, squirming as it did, until it encompassed all the floating parts. Held suspended above him, it looked like a large amniotic sac, writhing with movement, hands and legs pushing from inside, trying to get out. Then it burst, and a mix of blood and fluids covered Allen.

Rhonda, blood-soaked and gasping, hovered before him, whole again. Reaching for Allen, she kissed him, and he returned the gesture, pulling her close. Rhonda wrapped her legs around him and thrust her hips into his. They made love to each other, rolling sensually through the air.

Rebecca stood below them, holding her hands above her head, laughing and dancing with glee.

Chapter Nine

Hide and Seek

When Rhonda and Allen left the mine, the night was full upon them. The moon had dropped below the hill and the clouds had dissipated, leaving the vast fog of the Milky Way stretching in splendor across the night sky. But they paid little attention to it. The two were on fire, finding it difficult to keep their hands off one another.

The motor home was empty. Sage had mysteriously vanished, to where Rhonda didn't care. They showered and got dressed again, but not before another love making session. But even with the expended energy, they were ready for more excitement.

Rebecca's voice loomed heavily in Allen's mind. He felt it more than heard it, growing stronger since his transformation. He separated his parts from his body for a moment, per her instructions, then, with a lot of concentration, brought them back together. At first, he didn't want to. He wanted to fly away and enjoy the new sensations, but she urged him to come back.

The craziest part of all was her declaration of his promotion to her greatest general of all time. It was more than he could comprehend, but the power did surge in him. There was no doubt he was feeling something. More troubling though was the girl he'd seen in the mines.

He didn't know who she was, but there was an obvious connection, like he should know her. But the more he tried to focus on her, the more Rebecca's voice took over. Rebecca's power surged in him, and he needed a release, or he felt he would explode.

"What do we do now? I need to do something. I feel like I can't sit still, like I want to separate and fly into the night."

"Completely normal feeling. I wanted to the first time I became part of the collective. To serve Rebecca, though, is a much bigger high. Let's get out of here and go someplace to let off some steam. Samson's waiting by the tent with the car."

"How do you know?"

"We have a thing, kind of a connection. It's called a cell phone, silly."

Allen smirked, then chased Rhonda out the door, catching her just before she got to the car. He grabbed her by the wrist and turned her to him. In response, she pulled loose and, with unbelievable quickness, jumped on his back, playfully nibbling his ear. He grabbed her, turned her, then pinned her against the closed car door, grinding his hips to her mid-section. She gave in to his playful assault, wrapping her legs around him, pulling him closer to her. She kissed him deeply as he touched her breasts.

"My, aren't you the eager one?" she said.

Allen released her for a moment and opened the back door of the Cadillac. Rhonda scampered inside and pulled him in on top of her. Allen rolled into the seat beside her and got comfortable as Rhonda straddled him. Reaching into her pocket, she retrieved a dime bag of weed.

"Would you like some?" She waved the bag teasingly in front of him.

"Of course. Pot always makes me horny."

She massaged his very present erection through the fabric of his pants. "I don't think you need any help. Samson?"

"Yes, Rhonda?" the big man said from the driver's seat.

"Where's the nearest place we can go dancing?"

"I believe an establishment called Pa-Rudy's exists a mere fifteen minutes from here. Will it do?"

"Absolutely! Let's go, but first, stop at a gas station so I can pick up some rolling papers."

Samson started the car and pulled onto the highway. Peering in the rear- view mirror for a moment, he regarded the couple in the back seat, mostly unclothed already, and smiled.

Driving up and down Main Street, Sy checked every haunt he could think of, but still no sign of Allen. It would be much easier if he knew the car his son was driving, or, as Sy thought may be the case, if he was on foot. The latter made no sense, though. If he was, they'd surely find him quickly. He thought, even though Allen had been gone from town for a while, he still knew people. He had some of his old friends running around. Maybe one of them had seen him.

Patty continued to drink and, at the pace she was going, wouldn't be much help. But two sets of eyes, even if they were blurry ones, was still better than one. They also drove by the Owens farm and saw the tent, stalwart and defiant to any norm of the town, but still no sign of them.

"Where could they be?" Sy said, the frustration evident in his voice.

"Maybe they left town? You don't think they would go back to Lexington, do you?"

"By now, it's possible. But I don't think so. I have a feeling they're close. Don't ask me why."

"Hey, Sy, is there some kind of hangout in town? Where younger people gather?"

"Not really. The coffee shop maybe. What time is it?"

Patty checked her watch, the digital display flashed. "Eight o'clock."

"It'll be closing in about an hour. We'll head there."

Moments later, Sy pulled his car into the strip mall with the Mountain Perk logo on the end. All the other stores were closed except the dollar store, always a destination for last minute shoppers in the evening.

Sy went inside the coffee shop where a boy and a girl, much younger than Allen, were cleaning behind the counter. He strolled to the bar. "Can I get a cup of coffee, please?"

The girl stepped to the register. "Sure, do you want a regular or latte?"

Sy, confused at what the latter was, said, "Regular, I suppose. Hey, you didn't happen to see a couple of kids come by here earlier, a few years older than you, a man about five-foot-ten with black hair and a girl about five-foot-four and red hair?"

"I remember them. They were by this morning. The girl assaulted one of our workers."

"Really? Who was the worker?"

"Nathan McCarthy. He didn't deserve it, though. He was only asking about the guy, trying to catch up on old times."

Nathan McCarthy? One of Henry's boys. The main antagonist at the funeral. He could always manage to stir up shit, but unless his brother Jesse backed him up, he couldn't dish it out.

"Did you see where they went?"

"No. They got into a big, old black car, like a limousine or something, and took off."

Sy immediately thought of the Cadillac that had followed him home from Lexington. *Could it be, and why?*

The girl slid his coffee to him and said, "That'll be two ninety-five."

Three bucks for a small cup of coffee? Damn highway robbery. Moe's gas station only charged ninety-nine cents, and Sy usually got his for free. He reluctantly paid for his coffee, nodded at the girl, and returned to Patty.

"Did they see them?" she asked.

"Yeah, earlier today. Said they were riding around in a Cadillac, a big one, like a limo."

"Strange. Where would Rhonda find a limo? She's only a nurse and doesn't make enough to afford something like that."

"I don't know, but it makes me wonder what kind of shit they're mixed- up in." He shook his head. "We've been all around this town and haven't seen a thing, which makes me think they've left already. When we drove by the tent earlier, did you notice a car there?"

"No."

"Neither did I. The car I saw coming home from Lexington matched the description of the car the girl in there told me about, and it was parked by the tent earlier today. Somethings up, and I don't like it, especially if my sons involved. Maybe I should call Sally and see if she's seen him." Sy reached into his pocket for his cell phone before realizing it was on the nightstand by his bed. "Damn. I left it at home."

"We could use mine, if you want," Patty said.

"No, it would confuse her when she didn't see me calling. I'll wait until I get home to call her. For now, we can go to Moe's. He should be open. Find out if he's seen anything."

"Good." Patty giggled, raising the half full jar of shine for a drink. "I have to pee."

Sy smiled and started the car. He pulled out of the parking lot and onto the highway. As he drove, he started thinking about what Sally would say if she knew he was running around town with a girl ten years younger than him? What would Moe, an old friend and drinking buddy of his, say?

Hell, he'd probably be impressed. But the town will talk. I guess they would anyway, once they found out she was staying at his house.

He was too far in to care at that point. So much had happened in the previous days with Allen and all. No amount of town gossip could faze him.

When they pulled into Moe's, Patty opened the door before he came to a complete stop and stumbled out.

Great, not only do I have a woman with me, but a drunk one. Moe's gonna laugh his ass off.

He opened the door of the gas station, letting Patty go before him.

"Thank you, you're a true gentleman." Patty turned to a heavy, bearded man behind the counter. "Where's your bathroom?

The man pointed toward the back of the store. Moe Spencer watched as Patty walked by, his eyes trailing to her bottom.

"Mm, mmm." He shook his head and smiled at her, his red gums showing a mouth void of teeth. Patty gave him a disgusted look and hurried back to the lady's room.

Grabbing a bottle of water from the cooler, Sy walked to the counter where a grinning Moe Spencer greeted him.

"Damn, Sy. You, old dog. Who's the fine piece of ass with you?"

"C'mon, Moe, it ain't like that. She was my son's nurse, one of them anyway, while he was in the hospital. The other has been taking care of Allen since I got him home."

"I heard you had a nurse stayin' with ya. But you sayin' you got two of 'em now? Damn, you are one lucky son of a bitch."

"Unlucky's more like it. It's been nothing but crazy since Allen's been home. It's all the same. Try not to let Sally know I'm with a woman. She worries about me too much as it is. Rhonda, the nurse who helped Allen recover, left somewhere with him. They haven't been in here, have they?"

"I saw Allen about half an hour ago, looking pretty good for a man who just got out of the hospital. He was with a red head. Pretty and built like a brick shithouse. Your boy must have a big pecker to get a piece of action like her!" Moe grinned.

"I wish it were just for his anatomy. I think she has other reasons."

"Aww shit. She ain't got him hooked on heroin, does she? My sister's on that shit. Ambulance had to dose her with Narcan the other day, got so bad. Damn near lost her. My momma checked her into rehab. Guarantee she'll be back on when she gets out, though. Can't get that monkey off your back."

"I don't know what he's on, Moe."

"The girl bought some rolling papers. Maybe they'd been to see ole Buck?"

"Anything's possible right now. They didn't happen to say where they were going?"

"Naw. But they looked chummy, if you know what I mean," Moe gave Sy a wink. "Got into a big Cadillac. An old one, big enough to be a limo, but not stretched or anything. Someone you know?"

"No, but I feel they're up to no good. Did you see the direction they were going?"

"Looked like they were headed out Route 8, maybe to the county line? I'd say Pa-Rudy's if I were guessing right. Good place to take a lady, but it can be a bit rowdy. Say, I know Nicole died in Lexington. Damn shame the way it happened, too. But don't you think Allen would still be grievin'? I mean, Nicole wasn't in the ground yet before he fell in the sink hole. Now, he's awake from a coma and with another girl? Don't seem like Allen."

Sy started to answer, but the door to the lady's room opened. Patty stumbled forward and steadied herself with Sy's shoulder.

"How's this ol' codger get a pretty thing like you to run around with him?"

"What makes you think it's not the other way around?" Patty winked.

"Damn, Sy! You got your hands full," Moe said, laughing.

Sy shook his head and put two dollars on the counter. "Keep the change, Moe. I'll talk to you later."

Sy helped Patty into the passenger seat. He was heading to the other side when he noticed Sheriff Oeny standing by his patrol car, waving him over. Ralph Oeny adjusted his belt, pulled his hat down in front, and walked toward Sy with the confidence of a man who was more federal agent than small town law man. Like his daddy before him, he took the job seriously.

"Evening to you, Ralph. How's your wife and kids?" Sy said.

"Everything's good with the family. I was just wondering if you'd seen your boy, Allen, in a while? There was a report of an assault on one of the McCarthy boys' over at the coffee house. There was a man and woman involved. The man fit Allen's description." He craned his neck to get a better look at Sy's passenger. "Who's your lady friend?"

"Patty Hudson. She was one of Allen's nurses who cared for him at the hospital in Lexington. She knows the woman with him. We've been all over town looking for them."

"Really? Who's the girl with Allen?"

"Her name's Rhonda Lane, and she was also a nurse taking care of Allen. I hired her to be his home health nurse, but it looks like things are becoming a bit more personal."

"Well, the report said she's the one who assaulted Nathan. Little punk probably had it coming, though. The call came in earlier, but I haven't heard anything since then. You think they may have left town?"

"Moe said the car they were in may have been headed to Pa-Rudy's"

"Of course it was. I go on more calls to that place than anywhere in this county, especially on Friday and Saturday nights. It's usually quiet on a weekday though."

"We may head that way ourselves soon. If we see him, I'll tell him you're looking for him. I'm sure he could clear everything up about the situation. Probably just a big misunderstanding."

"Allen's a good boy. I figure Nathan started the whole thing. But, still have to follow up. This whole town's going crazy right now with the tent revival and this magician fella running around. You know he's having a big to-do this Friday? I don't know if I have enough deputies to handle the crowd I know it's going to bring. Then, there's the escaped inmate on the loose. Some crazy from the state hospital. Doubt he'd come this far though."

Sy wondered if he should ask if the escapee matched the description of Harley but thought better of it. "Sounds like you've got your hands full."

"You don't know the half of it. Well, you see him, let me know. Good day to you, Sy."

"You, too. Tell Greta I said hi."

Sheriff Oeny nodded and got in his car, waving as he pulled out of Moe's parking lot. Sy opened his car door and found Patty sleeping in the seat, the jar, one drink left, tilting from its perch between her legs. Good thing the sheriff didn't look inside the car, he thought. Sy reached to grab it before it fell and hesitated nervously at the thought of putting his hands near another woman's body. *What would Sadie think?* Of course, the answer was nothing. She was dead, but still, he had reservations.

The jar released from the grasp of her thighs, and in a knee jerk reaction, Sy was able to grab it, grazing her bare skin with his hand as he did. The motion sent a shock through him he hadn't felt in quite some time. Patty, curvy in all the right places, was a looker, but she liked girls. So, any notions, as misguided as they probably would be, were for nothing. It was time to get his head back on the mission, finding Allen before he got into trouble.

He pulled onto the highway and headed for the edge of the county, to Pa-Rudy's.

Chapter Ten

Sins

P a Rudy's was hopping with loud country music. It was only Thursday, but the weekend crowd had come early. The parking lot was full and lit up with not only streetlamps but a spotlight beaming into the dark sky, moving erratically in different directions. The name of the establishment was written in large, illuminated letters on the roof as well as on two large banners announcing various specialties the bar was known for, one being dancing.

The whole place looked like an oasis in the middle of nowhere. All of Salt Flat and the surrounding towns seemed to have descended there, evident by the number of cars filling the lot. A good amount of alcohol would be flowing, legal and not so legal, as well as any drug you could get your hands on, the perfect place for two young people with energy to spare.

Samson pulled the Cadillac in front of the building, then opened the door for Rhonda and Allen. Patrons standing around outside were visibly impressed as Rhonda stepped from the car, staring wide-eyed at the bar. Allen followed.

"This place is alive," Rhonda said.

"It's grown since the last time I was here. They must've added on."

Rhonda considered what he said. "Are you remembering things now?"

Allen smiled. "Only the good things. I could care less about anything else. Are you ready to go in?"

Allen did feel good, better than he ever had, ready to take on anything coming his way. The attire they wore, courtesy of Rhonda, was appropriate for the place: blue jeans and a button up shirt for Allen, tight pants with frayed rips down the front showing just the right amount of leg for Rhonda. She also wore a button up blouse, open enough in the front to see a wife-beater style t-shirt underneath, tight with an ample amount of cleavage showing. They both had boots on as required by the establishment.

Strolling past a few smokers scattered on either side of the entrance, Allen opened the double doors for Rhonda, and they entered the building. A large bald man with a black beard was standing inside the door, checking I.D.'s. He asked for theirs, and Rhonda giggled.

"Something funny, ma'am?"

"No, just feels good to be carded. Hasn't happened to me in a while."

"I would think a fine thing like you would be too young not to get asked." He looked at Allen. "Better watch her close."

Allen held Rhonda's hand to lead her through the crowd to a table near the bar. A waitress in a tight shirt and jeans came to take their order.

"What can I get you folks?" she said.

"I'll have a vodka and cranberry juice. What about you, Allen?"

"Miller Lite is fine."

People were crowded onto a dance floor in front of a small stage where a band by the name of Possum Spit played covers of various country music hits. Wannabe cowboys were mixed with rednecks and girls with too much makeup.

"Let's dance, Allen. I'm feeling good! How about you?" Rhonda yelled over the din of the music.

"Great! I've never had so much energy."

The waitress returned with their drinks, and Rhonda dug into her pocket to retrieve a credit card.

"Open a tab?" the waitress asked.

Rhonda nodded, and grabbed Allen's hand. Allen downed half his glass and followed her to the dance floor. They two-stepped to a George Strait tune with a few other couples joining in.

After the song was over, they turned to go back to their table. As the crowd parted to let them through, they were surprised by a guy leaning on their table, drinking a beer. He had a mullet haircut hanging to the middle of his back over a shirt with cut out sleeves, muscles bulging, farm-type muscles. Hard work was no stranger to him.

"Allen Sutton! When the fuck did you get back to town? Last I heard, you was in the crazy hospital with the rest of the looney tunes! Now, I see you here. Who would of thought?"

"Do you know this guy, Allen?"

"You look familiar, but I don't think I know you," Allen said to the man.

"The fuck you talkin' about? You know me. Jesse McCarthy, Nicole's brother. Don't tell me you done forgot about her, too? After what you did to her, you got some big balls showing up here!"

"We're here to dance and have a good time, buddy. Allen doesn't know you, and he had nothing to do with your sister's death. Now, get the hell out of here!"

"You always let your woman talk for you, Sutton? Real nice and all, how you've moved on after you killed Nicole. I wish you'd died in that hole. You're a worthless piece of shit, Sutton!" Jesse retorted.

"Allen. Let's leave, forget this redneck."

Allen considered Jesse for a moment. He had to admit, he did look familiar. Since they'd left the mine, his head was becoming clearer, but all things save Rebecca seemed unimportant. He could feel her presence all around him. Rhonda was still his girlfriend, but Rebecca held a fascination he couldn't contain.

Absorbed in his thoughts of her, he almost didn't see the fist coming at him. He moved his head slightly, and Jesse missed Allen's jaw by a millimeter.

The crowd around them was backing up, forming a circle, preparing for the fight to come. Anyone would assume Jesse, five inches taller than Allen and looking much meaner, would be the victor in the fight, but Allen didn't move, only stared him down. Another guy, the one Rhonda hit between the legs earlier in the day, stepped next to Jesse.

"Hey, brother? This guy giving you trouble?"

"I got this, Nathan. Get back to the bar."

"Hey, aren't you the guy we saw at the coffee shop earlier today?" Rhonda said.

Nathan instinctively put his hand to his crotch to avoid another stray kick.

"Oh yeah, it's you all right." Rhonda laughed.

Allen heard some of the conversation between Rhonda and Nathan but was more intent on backing down Jesse, whose face was still like a poker shark. Except Jesse wasn't bluffing; he meant to take Allen apart.

"This has been a long time comin', Sutton," Jesse said.

"That's enough!" A bouncer, cued by the circled crowd, pushed his way through the tight group around Allen and Jesse and stepped between them. "You need to take it outside, or I'll toss all of ya out!"

"Randy Lynch. Who the fuck died and made you boss?" Jesse said.

"I'm not afraid of you like everybody else is around here. You remember how I sacked you in football, don't you? Well, I can still do it. Now, you want to fight? Get outside."

Jesse stared Randy down, the scowl on his face suggesting it wasn't close to being over. He scoffed, then turned to Allen. "How about it? We goin' out back to take care of this, or you goin' back to Salt Flat like the chicken shit ya are?"

"Oh, I'm going outside," Allen said.

Rebecca says I am. She needs soldiers. The thought jumped into his head, strong, more like a command. A devious smile appeared on Rhonda's face, indicating she knew exactly what he was thinking.

"Allen? Are you ready to do what needs to be done?"

A confident smile fell across Allen's face. "Don't worry. I know what Rebecca needs."

Looming large between them, the bouncer waited impatiently for a decision. Jesse, joined by Nathan, turned for the back door.

"Show's over, folks! Get back to dancing!" The bouncer bellowed as he walked away, waving his hands over his head.

Allen moved to follow the McCarthy boys outside while Rhonda closed her tab. She retrieved her cell phone from her purse and made a call.

The alley in the back was empty. Nights at Pa Rudy's usually included a fight or two, typically starting inside the bar, garnering the attention of the crowd. But once it spilled into the alley, no one gave it another look.

"Looks like your girlfriend left you. Maybe when I'm done, I'll go show her a good time. How about it, Nate? You up for some pitty pussy tonight? We can both have a turn at her." Jesse sneered and turned his attention to Allen.

Allen never flinched, only smiled. Jesse swung wildly in the air, throwing a few near misses to test Allen's resolve. He became visibly frustrated that he wasn't doing much to unnerve his opponent and swung directly at Allen's face.

Instead of connecting though, Allen easily grabbed the McCarthy boy's hand, bending it backward, causing Jesse to howl in pain.

Nervously looking at his hand, Jesse tried to awkwardly deliver another punch with his free hand. It was done mostly out of instinct, but it did no good. He couldn't muster the strength and dropped to his knees instead.

"Let go, you motherfucker!" he screamed, but Allen didn't.

Allen bent the wrist farther, twisting as he did, snapping the bones before releasing Jesse to writhe on the pavement. Allen started toward him to finish the deed when Nathan, who'd been nervously watching, waiting for the opportunity to jump in, decided that was it.

Running headlong at Allen, Nathan attempted to football tackle him. A poor choice, because instead of wrapping Allen at the waist as he intended to do, Nathan was sent sprawling downward as Allen used the force of his momentum against him. Blood spurted from Nathan's nose, his face making contact with the hard pavement.

Allen turned his attention back to Jesse and smiled as the man cowered against the exterior of Pa Rudy's with tears streaming down his face, begging for mercy. The power Allen felt was an aphrodisiac as Rebecca's presence surged within him.

Soldiers, Allen. We need soldiers! Her voice echoed in his mind.

Grabbing Jesse's mangled wrist, Allen twisted, forcing him to stand. With his free hand, he made a fist, aimed at Jesse's solar plexus, and rammed it through. Allen's hand came out the other side, holding the beating heart of Jesse McCarthy.

The look on Jesse's face was sheer terror and shock as he screamed, gurgling and spitting blood at the same time. Allen pulled the organ back through the chest cavity and held it where Jesse could see.

Allen bit into it.

Tears fell from Jesse's eyes, and his body trembled. As Allen lowered him to the ground.

The pain in Jesses face released, and his eyes focused on something in the distance. Somehow, he was not yet dead but also not quite alive.

A woman came into his sight, dark skinned, dark eyes, and hair raven black. Blood dripped from her mouth, falling over her naked body. She beckoned to Jesse, and he obliged, breathing his last.

Nathan, who was rebounding from the last attack, watched in bewilderment. His brothers body lay there in the alleyway, bloodied, a hole in his chest. Jesse's insides were strewn on the pavement. Nathan gasped and vomited the contents of his stomach. Coming up for breath, he screamed at Allen.

"You're dead, you son of a bitch!"

Pulling the gun he'd tucked in his jeans, the one he never used except for show, Nathan leveled it at Allen's head and fired. Three rounds emptied from the Glock, as fast as he could pull the trigger. Instead of hitting Allen's head, though, the first bullet entered his shoulder, the second through his neck, and the third in his upper arm, causing him to flinch. But Allen didn't go down, only stood there, gazing at Nathan with wild eyes.

Nathan looked at him, puzzled, unsure how Allen was still standing. With a crazed scream, he emptied the rest of the bullets into Allen's body.

Allen smiled, his mouth widening as he did until his jaws cracked, dislocating from their intended place on his face. Several rows of teeth appeared in Allen's mouth.

Nathan screamed as Allen reached for him, grasping the front of his shirt and lifting him into the air. Then, Allen bit into Nathan's neck, removing a large piece of flesh. Blood jutted in great streams, spraying onto Allen's face. Nathan screamed again as he struggled to free himself, but Allen's grip was too tight; he had no chance of getting loose.

In one quick movement, Allen pushed Nathan McCarthy onto the outside wall of the bar. Music pulsed from inside and the wall vibrated.

"This is the luckiest day of your life. Rebecca needs you!" Allen said in a raspy voice as he dug into Nathan's chest.

Nathan tried to cry out, but he only made a gurgling sound. Bone cracked, and Nathan's sternum gave way to Allen's hand as he gripped the heart inside Nathan's chest. Pulling it free, Allen bit into it, consuming the dark red organ in one satisfying chomp.

Blood dripped from the mouth of Nathan McCarthy and the light in his eyes began to fade. But before it did, he saw Jesse walking behind Allen, his body healing itself.

The alleyway faded away, and a beautiful woman, dark and bloody, came into view. A realization washed over Nathan. He wasn't dying. Actually, he never felt so alive.

Rhonda stepped out the back door just in time to see Jesse go down, and she watched intently as Allen dispatched Nathan. Pleased with Allen's ferocity, she smiled, sure Rebecca would be happy as well.

"Allen, we have to get out of here!"

He licked the blood from his fingers, lowered Nathan to the ground and looked at her as if she were insane.

"Why the hurry?"

Rhonda started to answer but looked at the scene instead. Jesse was wandering around the alley, dazed and confused but beginning to gather his wits about him. The massive amount of blood on the ground or the blood stains on Allen's shirt couldn't be hidden.

Rebecca had a plan for him, and although she'd welcome the new converts, Allen couldn't be seen there. If the authorities got involved, it would slow Rebecca's plan. Rhonda had to get him away. Samson was on his way, and they needed to get to the front of the building to catch a ride.

Nathan stirred on the ground, coming to and would be able to stand shortly.

"Whew! I don't know what you did to me, Sutton, but I feel better than I ever have. I'm ready to go party."

"No. Not now. We have to go. Trust me, there'll be time later. We have to get back to the tent before the police arrive," Rhonda said.

Allen gave her a puzzled look. "Why?"

"Because Rebecca isn't ready to be revealed. Let's go."

Helping Nathan to his feet, Jesse steadied him and turned to follow Allen and Rhonda. They disappeared from the alley and got into a waiting Cadillac Fleetwood in front of the building.

Shortly after, a couple wandered outside to the back of the bar in for a little one on one time. Before they could get their clothes loose, though, they both realized they were standing in a pool of blood. Pieces of flesh and bone fragments were strewn in with the mix. More blood was splattered on the wall, like some morose painting. The girl screamed.

"101? Are you there 101? Over," the radio in Ralph Oeny's car squawked.

He keyed the microphone. "I'm here, Carla. What's you got for me?"

"We've got a signal seven over at Pa-Rudy's. Bill's there. He says there's blood everywhere. Over."

Bill Pence? Ralph wondered how much of the evidence his deputy had already tampered with. The man meant well but wasn't always the most professional.

"Do they have anybody apprehended?"

"No. Nobody was there when he arrived. No bodies, just a girl who noticed all the blood. Said it looked like a war zone."

"I'm on my way. Should be there in three minutes."

"I'll let him know. Over."

"Over and out," Ralph said.

"Ten-four, Ralph. Be careful." Carla said, then radio silence.

A few minutes later, Ralph pulled into the parking lot of Pa Rudy's. He adjusted his pants a little to allow his belly to settle over the gun belt, then snugged his hat on his head. As he entered the building, a large, bearded man greeted him, the bouncer he assumed.

"Hey, Sheriff. If you're looking for the deputy, he's in back of the building where all the blood was found."

"Yeah, I am. Tell me something though, you're the bouncer, right? Randy Lynch, all-state defensive end from Lee High School?"

"The same one."

"Really? Didn't you get a scholarship to UK?"

"Yeah, but it didn't last long. Blew my knee out my sophomore year, and now I'm here." Randy twirled his hand in the air.

"Tough break. Tell me though, did you happen to see any fights or anything? I figure this place has its share of them."

"The deputy asked the same thing. I told him there was an argument earlier in the evening. The McCarthy boys were involved. Looked like they were messing with a guy I didn't know. I told them to take it out back. I suppose it could have been them, but I wouldn't think a normal fight would produce so much blood. Plus, a few other things were found."

"Other things?"

"Yeah, pieces that should stay inside the body. If you know what I mean," Randy said.

"Got it. Nice talking to you." Ralph walked toward the back door.

Most of the bar was empty, save a few who'd drank so much they'd need a cab. Ralph stepped out the back door and saw Bill crouched down in the middle of the alley, a trail of smoke from the cigarette in his mouth lifting into the air like a chimney above him.

Ralph shook his head. Bill stood in a pool of blood. Police tape had been placed across the entrance and exit of the alleyway, and the metal hand railing on the steps. Ralph stretched the yellow plastic barrier over his head and made his way to his deputy.

"Hey, Bill. What's you got here?"

"Hi, Ralph." Bill stood and stretched.

He was a tall, lanky man with leathery skin, deep lines around his eyes, and a tuft of gray hair. Ralph outweighed him by about fifty pounds, but it wasn't always so. Bill had been much heavier, but after a bout of lung cancer, he was a shell of his former self. He still smoked, even though the doctors told him it would kill him someday.

Most with weaker resolve would've stopped working, but not Bill. He'd be walking the beat until he fell over dead. The stress of the job coupled with his smoking habit would see to it.

Talking from the side of his mouth, the cigarette in the other corner, Bill said, "Looks like a homicide to me. I'd say the boys in forensics will want to take a look."

Ralph shook his head, knowing as well as Bill did they didn't have such a thing in Salt Flat. "If you mean the coroner, then I figure he's on his way. Carla should have called him by now. Only thing is, where are the bodies?"

"Damned if I know. When I got here, a girl and her boyfriend were standing right about where you are now. I took a statement and let her go. She saw what we're seeing now, a bunch of blood and guts, but no bodies. Now, when that bouncer in there, the one who went all-state in football, came out here, he helped me find more guts over there." Bill pointed to the other side of the alley. "That boy's not squeamish at all. But someone like him has probably seen his share of blood."

Ralph sighed and wondered why Bill would let Randy out there at all. The lack of professionalism was hard to fathom, but it was Bill after all. Ralph stared at the blood. "I wonder if someone hid the bodies in a car or something to bury in a shallow grave somewhere else? The bouncer said he thought the McCarthy boys may be involved. They were harassing someone earlier."

A thought occurred to him. Nathan McCarthy was involved in the altercation earlier at the coffee shop. Maybe he'd followed Allen out there, but that would mean Jesse was probably involved too.

"What are you thinking, Ralph?"

"I'm thinking we need to clean this mess up. The coroner can take a look but won't be able to do much with the scene the way it is. I think our best course of action is to go see Henry McCarthy and ask if he's seen his boys tonight."

"Sounds like a good idea. He may know something. Lead the way and I'll follow."

"Bill, I need you to stay here for when the coroner shows up. Let him know what's going on. I'll go see Henry myself."

***

"How much farther to the bar, Sy?" Patty said. "I have to pee again."

"We should be there soon, about five minutes or so."

Sy looked at the speedometer and saw they were going sixty. He could probably have gone a little faster but didn't want to get pulled over by a stray state cop running the road.

Suddenly, lights blinded him from a car coming around the corner, half in their lane and half in his. Sy swerved to miss them, running onto the shoulder of the road. The vibration of rumble strips ran through the car, causing Patty to jump. His eyes widened.

The Cadillac.

Locking the brakes, Sy's car skidded to a stop.

"Damn, too late. I peed!"

Sy saw the dark spot between her legs. Good thing his car had leather seats.

"Don't worry about it. We have to turn around anyway."

"Why? What about the bar?"

"It can wait. I doubt they're there. I just saw the Cadillac go by. The girl at the coffee shop said they got into it, so they must be going back home."

Patty turned her head to look out the window in the wrong direction. "Oh, good."

Sy veered into the lane going back to Salt Flat and followed a good distance behind the car.

"You're a good man, Sy Sutton. I don't know why I didn't see it before, back at the hospital anyway."

He smiled. "It's okay. I didn't give you much reason to trust me. I'm glad you decided to be my partner in crime tonight. Hopefully, we'll get some answers."

He readjusted in the seat and gave her hand a gentle pat. She surprised him by putting her head on his shoulder. He thought about protesting but didn't. He liked it.

Chapter Eleven

The Sins of the Fathers

After giving instruction to Bill for the coroner, Ralph tugged on his pants and turned to leave.

A man shuffled toward them, police tape wrapped around his body, obviously ignoring the barrier. The yellow stood out from his dirty white shirt with the large black letters, "LMH", printed on it.

Ralph put a hand on his pistol and sized up the man. Skinny and poor looking, hair disheveled, and wild eyes glowing in the darkness. Ralph figured it was the escapee from the mental hospital in Lexington.

But how the hell did he get here?

Ralph wouldn't wait to see. He thought the man would be in a body bag if he took one step closer.

"State your business, buddy."

Tilting his head sideways, the way a dog does when curious, the man said, "She crawls from below the earth and seeks to find that which is hers. She calls to all of us, and we the sheep respond. Are you worthy? Are you?"

"What the hell?" Ralph glanced over at Bill, who had his hand on his pistol as well. "Listen, buddy, we don't want any trouble. Don't give us a reason to shoot. Come with us, and we'll get you back to where you came from."

"I came out of the box for her, and I'll go back as soon as her mission is complete. You would, too, if you understood the power she gives. I smelled the blood of the soldiers and came this way. Where are they?"

Ralph watched as Bill crept closer, drawing his gun. Ralph gestured to him, shaking his head side to side, but Bill ignored him and went forward anyway. The man didn't flinch, even though he spotted Bill coming his way. When Bill was within three feet of the man, he pulled his weapon the rest of the way from its holster.

"Cease and desist. You're under arrest."

The man smiled unwaveringly toward the gun, showing no fear. He reached for Bill and the deputy fired. Ralph immediately pulled his gun and ran toward the man, both outstretched hands on the weapon in case his deputy hadn't completely dispatched the perpetrator. But instead of lying on the ground, the man was still standing.

"The hell?" Ralph said.

Bill, who still had his gun drawn, fired again and again, emptying all six rounds of his .38 Special into the gut of the assailant.

The man considered him for a moment then lunged forward, striking Bill in the chest. Ralph heard his deputy cry out for one brief moment, but the sound was quickly replaced with the bubbling of blood in Bill's throat. Bone cracked, and the deputy's insides gushed in a torrent from his back as the wild man's hand exploded outward, holding the deputy's heart.

Speechless, his hands shaking, the gun jumping erratically, Ralph tried to get a bead on him, but he couldn't keep his hand steady. The man held the organ in his hand before pulling it back through the chest cavity, snapping ribs as he did. Bill's body crumbled to the ground, the look on his face sheer terror at the suddenness of the assault to his body.

The man grinned and crushed the pulpy black muscle in his hand. Ralph stared in disbelief, fighting to keep his dinner down, the vomit burning in his throat.

"Stop what you're doing, and step away from that man, or I'll shoot!"

Behind him, the door to the bar flung open, and Randy walked out. Seeing the man, then the blood bath before him, he said, "Holy shit. What the fuck is going on?"

Ralph waved him back inside, but Randy stood there, eyes wide at the sight in front of him. Ralph trained his gun on the man, firing repeatedly. The bullets, same as before, had no effect on him. He watched in disbelief as the man began to fall apart. His arms first then his legs broke free from his body and hovered in the air. His torso and head launched upward into the night sky. The appendages floated for a moment before following the rest of the body.

Ralph fell to his knees, his legs unable to hold him anymore. His whole body was a mass of goose-bumped flesh, and the ability to talk had left him.

"Sheriff? Did you see that? Tell me you saw that?"

Ralph said nothing to him, only watched with wide eyes as his old friend lay mutilated in front of him.

Sy drove far enough behind the Cadillac to avoid detection, watching as it turned into the Owen's farm where the tent was erected. He slowed down but didn't turn in behind them. Instead, he continued along the highway, pulling off the road a short distance ahead and turning off the headlights.

"We'll wait here for a minute, then turn back," he said to Patty.

"Do you think Allen and Rhonda are with him?"

"I don't know what to think right now, Patty, but I need to know what's going on."

"I don't like this. My pants are wet, and I'm out of moonshine."

"It won't take long," he reassured her.

From their vantage point, they could see the tent and the camper behind it. The Cadillac was parked beside the camper, and the motorhomes inside lights were on.

"I wonder what they're doing?" Patty said.

"I don't know. But if nothing happens soon, we need to go before someone notices us."

The lights in the camper went off, and the door opened. Six people walked out. A tall, skinny man who Sy figured to be the Sage walked in front with a large man who Sy assumed to be the Sage's bodyguard. Allen, Rhonda, and the McCarthy boys were in the rear. Sy was surprised to see Allen with them, based on the past animosity he received from the McCarthy's. Yet there they all looked like friends. The group entered the tent and disappeared.

"What do you think? Should we go over there?" Patty said.

"No. I think we should wait, see if Allen and Rhonda come back to my place tonight. I don't know what this guy is up to, but I'm thinking it's no good. Besides, if we go over there now, we would technically be trespassing, and by looking at the bunch with them, I don't think we'd be welcome."

"All right. Your call. I'm tired anyway." Patty yawned.

Sy headed for home, hoping Allen would make it there too.

Faint light illuminated inside the tent as the blue flame consistently burned. The body parts could be heard high above. A cacophony of voices, buzzing in unison. Sitting cross legged, her head leaned forward against a small stage on the opposite end of the floor, was Rebecca. She wore no clothing. Reminiscent of an Egyptian princess, she radiated all manner of sin. She raised her head in their direction, and summoned Allen, Rhonda, and the McCarthy boys with only her mind. The parts above moved faster, producing a louder hum of excitement, as her telepathy reached them, too. Once the four were in front of her, she spoke.

"Allen, my general, you've done well. More soldiers to carry out my bidding. We will summon others before the night is done, and they will come here to be part of the collective." Rebecca raised her hands to the ceiling as the parts became more excited from her revelation of newcomers. She smiled, then looked toward the entrance of the tent. As if on cue, the flaps opened, and in walked a disheveled man with blood splattered across his dirty white shirt, the letters "LMH" on the front. Everyone turned to see the guest.

"Harley. Welcome back," Rhonda said. "I see the concoction I injected in you was enough to get you back to us and back to your old self."

He bowed. "Yes, it was, thank you."

"Do you have anyone for me?"

Harley, his hair stringy and sticking out in all directions, pulled together the best cordiality he could and knelt on one knee.

"Sorry, my queen, but the one I tried to convert was too close to death already. His insides were charred with disease, too unsavory for the collective."

"Well, too bad then, but don't worry. There will be others." She glanced toward Samson. "Prepare the car. Tonight, we hunt. We'll take our new converts to see what they can do. Harley? Will you join us too?"

"Yes, my queen, but if it's all the same, I'd prefer to go to town alone as cars give me the willies."

"As you wish." She looked upward and raised her hands. "Come, my children."

At the sound of her voice, the parts swooped from their perch above, rotating in a large circle around the flame, and took a hovering position in front of her. Arms, legs, torsos, and heads, chattering noisily in the air.

"Don't worry my children," said Rebecca, "there will be plenty for you to do soon. The revival is coming, and you will have lots of bodies to choose from. Be patient."

They continued to levitate for a moment before returning to the top of the tent.

Allen watched in amazement, possibly recognizing one of the heads as an old friend of his dad's. Buck, he thought his name was.

Oh well, looks like he's in good company now.

The engine revved outside, and Sage brought a silk robe for Rebecca. He placed it over her shoulders, holding it to allow her to put her arms through. She pulled her hair from under the garment, and when she flipped her head side to side, the hair fell into perfect symmetry. She cinched the robe at her waist and walked outside with the rest following her. Harley launched himself into the night.

Sage held Rebecca's hand until she was seated in the Cadillac. He closed the door, as the rest of the group got in on the other side.

Allen looked around in awe at the vastness of the vehicle. It seemed to have grown larger since he and Rhonda last rode in the back seat. The McCarthy boys didn't seem to notice, only sat smugly like a couple of wannabe gangsters ready to knock somebody off.

Allen leaned closer to Rhonda. "Has the car gotten bigger or is it just me?"

"This car accommodates its size based on the number of occupants inside," Samson said from the driver's seat.

Rhonda grinned. "Exactly."

"What's it matter, Sutton? We're riding in high style now," Jesse said, Nathan nodding beside him.

"I guess you're right. It is pretty cool." Allen took Rhonda's hand, and she squeezed it back. His brow furrowed, as he noticed Jesse undressing her with his eyes. He thought about saying something, but saw Rhonda responding by biting her lip and giving him a wink.

Sage made his way toward the passenger seat but hesitated when he saw Sadie standing in the field near the tent. She smiled at him, then vanished.

The night before, he'd wandered through the same area, feeling her presence but never finding her. Why the curiosity over a ghost? Had he not seen his share of them over the years, every time the parts came back? But he had to admit, she was different.

He couldn't concern himself with those matters. Rebecca needed him to help her. He got into the car and made himself comfortable. He could feel Rebecca digging in his mind. She'd done it many times before, but for some reason, it didn't feel as smooth.

"Sage? What were you doing out there?"

He turned in the seat to look at her. "Nothing, my queen, why do you ask?"

She disregarded his question. "I find it strange I can't fully read your thoughts. You are becoming muddled to me. Is something happening I need to know about? You don't seem as focused."

"No, all is well," he said nervously.

Disdain dripped from her voice. "Good. Mind what you hear aside from me. Voices in the wind can corrupt the purest heart."

He smiled and looked out the window as the car moved along the gravel road leading to the highway.

When Sy and Patty returned to his trailer, she lay down on the couch while Sy, at her request, went to pour her another drink. By the time he brought it back, though, she was fast asleep, lightly snoring. Her pants were still wet, and he contemplated taking them off but thought better of it. Instead, he decided not to wake her and figured that, by the amount of the liquor she'd had, he wouldn't be able to anyway. The hangover she'd be nursing by morning would probably deter her from further excursions with Buck's good home brew, but maybe not. She seemed to be able to hold her drink pretty well.

He placed the remaining glass on the table next to his easy chair, then sat down. He considered her for a moment as she lay sleeping, pretty from head to toe in her jeans and t-shirt. Maybe he'd misjudged her. Despite his conflicted feelings, he couldn't complain having her beside him. She made him feel ten years younger.

Since their age difference was about the same, he should feel that way. Thoughts of Sadie came back to him as he remembered how she would fall asleep every night on the same couch. Most of the time, he laid a blanket over her and kissed her good night. Thinking about this made him realize he'd forgotten to cover Patty.

Standing from the easy chair, he made his way to the hall closet, and pulled one from the top shelf, a small throw blanket perfect for a summer night. He placed it gently over her and returned to the recliner. Sleeping in the easy chair probably wouldn't be the best for his back, but he felt it necessary to stay and keep an eye on her. He'd try and figure everything out in the morning, the sleeping arrangements among other things.

As he watched her peaceful slumber, his eyes began to get heavy and soon he was asleep.

####

The Cadillac rolled down Main Street, sleek and black, its tinted windows hiding the occupants. It pulled to a stop by the IGA, and Samson stepped out. He took a draw from his inhaler, then proceeded to open the back door for Rebecca and the rest of the group. No people were present, and the only light came from a nearby streetlamp. The town lay sleeping, innocently unaware of their presence.

"I feel many souls in need of release." Rebecca looked at Allen and the McCarthy's. "Gentlemen. Are you ready?"

"Yes, my queen," they said in unison.

"Good. Rhonda, go with them. We'll only take half the town now and the rest during the Revival."

Allen stepped beside her. "Why not just suck them dry and be done with it?"

"Because, my young general, too many at once is hard on the digestion, so to speak."

"Actually, hard to disseminate into the hive. All at once that is," Rhonda said.

"That's correct, my dear. Don't be so greedy, my eager boy. When they gather in the tent, the real fun will begin!"

Sage and Rebecca took one side of the street, and Rhonda, Allen, and the McCarthy's the other. Up ahead, Harley stepped from behind a building, then walked to join them.

In the shadows nearby, Reverend Mooney, the pastor of the only church in town, watched with interest. He'd been hearing about Sage, a revered and godly man who just showed up one day and had been systematically working on his congregation. Hypnotizing them, he thought.

Mooney had seen his type before. In fact, his grandfather called them snake oil salesmen, telling people what they wanted to hear instead of what they needed to know. In the past, many others had tried to set up shop in his town, and he always managed to convince the people of their ill intents. Once the other pastors figured they were getting nowhere, they usually settled outside of town in some rundown shack. That suited Mooney fine. Less riffraff he had to deal with. Sage was a different sort, though. It looked like they had some of the young men of the community following them, as well as some young girl he didn't know.

Wednesday was reserved for church. Reverend Mooney hadn't seen his usual members that night and was a little concerned. Would the people stop coming, instead to be lured by the charisma of the Sage and his magic tricks? It looked as though a pack of demons had descended upon his town. He watched as Henry McCarthy's boys made their way into Ralph Oeny's house. Mooney wondered where the sheriff could be. Greta should be home. Surely, she would call her husband.

What in heaven is happening? Then, another thought occurred to him. What if Sage had already convinced his congregation to follow?

He'd be out of a job, is what. The widow Jones wouldn't make her nightly visits if such a thing happened. Mooney loved those late night rendezvous. He would be sore if he had to miss them.

With his livelihood at stake, he did the only thing he knew to do, retreat into the shadows and run back to the church. He would call the sheriff's office and tell them about the shenanigans out there. They better listen to him, if they knew what was good for them. By God, he wouldn't lose his standing in the town. No dime store, snake oil preacher would dethrone him. He would see to it! He would have to make a surprise visit to this tent revival—don't think he wouldn't—and try to sway his followers away from this apostasy.

Sy woke to a knock on the door. He squinted through the slits of light streaming through the venetian blinds and raised his hand to shield his eyes. The noise from the other side of the door became more urgent and faster in tempo.

"Daddy? You in there? It's me, Sally."

"I'm coming!" He unlocked the door and eased it open, holding it from hitting the couch where Patty slept.

She stared at him, frustration apparent on her face. "How is Allen doing? You never called yesterday. Did you even have your phone with you?"

"Would you believe, I left it in the bedroom on the nightstand. Allen went out last night. I figured he'd be back by now."

Sy knew Sally wasn't the patient type, and he could tell she wasn't in a good mood. The strange car in the driveway probably wasn't helping either.

"Where's the nurse caring for him? Where have you been? And who's car is that?" She pointed to Patty's Toyota.

"Slow down. Come in, and I'll make coffee. Then I can tell you everything."

She exhaled an exasperated breath. "Okay. Let me tell Tom. He's waiting in the car. Says he has some errands to run. I'll stay here while he goes."

Sy watched her trot down the steps and over to the car. He could see the look of frustration in Tom's eyes, but he seemed to comply, and backed out of the driveway. As Sally walked past the Toyota, Sy saw her shake her head, then march toward the trailer.

"What's going on?" Patty said, rising from the couch. "I need some Ibuprofen. My head is splitting."

"My daughter Sally is here. You haven't met her yet, but I'll introduce you."

He turned toward her. His eyes widened, and his pulse rose. Patty was dressed in nothing but bra and panties. He looked away, clearly embarrassed.

"Your clothes?"

She reached for the blanket on the couch, covering herself the best she could.

"Oh, I'm sorry. I forgot I was undressed."

"Apparently you did."

Sy turned to see his red-faced daughter in the doorway. "Now, Sally. This isn't what it looks like."

She looked at Patty then at Sy, breathing in deep and exhaling loudly. Patty reached past Sy for her clothing on the floor. She gave a small wave. Sy realized so many lines had been crossed he'd never be able to fix them.

"Hi, I'm Patty. Pleasure to meet you. I'll excuse myself to the bathroom now." She backed away and turned to the hallway, exposing her backside and thong panties.

Sally shook her head and stared at her dad, who was taking in the view. "Dad? Can I talk to you on the porch?"

Sy knew he looked as though he'd been caught with his hand in the cookie jar, so he followed.

"Dad? What are you doing? Why is that girl here? Is she the reason you won't answer your phone? How old is she?"

"Sally, I'm not doing anything with her. She's a coworker of Rhonda's. I was out looking for Allen and Rhonda last night, and she was helping me. She didn't have anywhere else to go, so I put her up here."

"What do you mean, 'looking for Allen'? Where is he? He shouldn't be out on the town. Not so soon anyway. I mean, he was looking much better, but what if he has a relapse?"

"I know, he should have at least taken a few days off, but there appears to have been some potent stuff in the IV fluid that gave him the energy to go out. I left him for a bit. When I came back, he was gone and has been ever since. Even more, Patty checked out the bags of fluid and said it wasn't anything their hospital handed out. Strange thing though, it was made by the Pendleton Corporation. Same people I worked for."

"So, she gave him some kind of drugs? I've heard of new stuff on the street that makes people go off the deep end, and it's around here. Probably the Mexicans bringing it in. Tom says they can't build the wall fast enough. But this sounds bigger than some local drug dealer. If Pendleton Corp made it."

"I doubt the Mexicans have ever heard about this. If the cartels knew, they'd be trying to sell it by the cartons. Allen was up and about in only a few hours. Thing worrying me the most is they didn't come home last night but were spotted heading to Pa-Rudy's. We were going there to find them, but as I was driving, the Cadillac passed us. We followed and saw them, along with some others, going in the tent at the edge of town."

"The tent? A Cadillac? You need to fill me in. Why on earth would they go to the tent anyway?"

"I think they're mixed up with that preacher. The Sage, I think he's called. The people I talked to in town said they saw Allen and Rhonda getting in a Cadillac. The same one I saw parked by the tent. It pulled in there last night, so I pulled off the road a little ways and watched them. Sure enough, Allen and Rhonda got out, along with the McCarthy boys and some big fella. I didn't want to go over there in the dark, but I plan to go out there today and check things out."

"Henry's boys? I thought they hated Allen."

"It looks like they've made amends. The whole thing is crazy."

"Yes, it is, but Dad, I don't think it's a good idea to be messing around out there. I wonder if the Owens' know anything about Allen? Since they own the farm the tent's on, maybe they've seen something?"

Sy started to answer when Patty called through the door.

"Anybody for coffee? I started a pot."

"Good idea. Let's go back inside," Sy said.

Once inside, Sally sat down on one of the stools under the half bar separating the kitchen from the living room, and Sy on another. Patty had three mugs set up, the pumpkin creamer, and a half gallon of milk.

"Hope you don't mind, Sy. I went through your fridge and found this. This is my favorite creamer too."

"It's fine. Rhonda asked me to pick it up the other day. But you're welcome to it."

"Interesting. She never seemed to care for it at the hospital. Oh, and Sally, you have nothing to worry about with your dad and me. You see, I like girls."

Sally regarded her as if she was from another planet and helped herself to the milk, pouring a little into her mug. She slid it toward Patty for the coffee. After receiving the morning pick me up, she turned to Sy. "Now, dad, if you're set on going out to the Owens' farm, I think I should go with you. Myrtle Owens is a friend of mine. Eli and her boy play baseball together, and I've helped her with several fundraisers. Her boy's away for camp, but Bill's there with her. I know you know them, too, but not as well as I do. You go out there alone, and they might not be as welcoming."

"He won't be alone because I'm going too. I need to see what Rhonda is up to."

Sally cleared her throat and gave her dad a disapproving look.

He shook his head. "She's going, Sally. We're all in this together. She needs to find Rhonda like we do Allen."

"Okay, if you insist. But let me do the talking. Myrtle knows me well enough."

"All right, Sally, it's settled then. When Tom gets back, you can follow me and Patty out there."

Sally took a sip of coffee. Sy thought she looked as though she were sizing Patty up, and he wondered what was on her mind. Did she think Patty was a threat? Surely not. He settled on her being overly cautious. Why not? She had lost her mother and wasn't used to her dad having overnight guests, especially the female variety. Sy thought it best to tread lightly for a while.

"So, Patty, what's your interest in Rhonda?" Sally said.

"I was the head nurse at Lexington State Hospital where Allen was staying, and she was one of my floor nurses. The night Sy took Allen,

Rhonda had done a few things I thought out of sort, and I thought maybe Allen could be in trouble. So, I came out here to help in any way I could. When I got here, I found Rhonda had beat me to it. Now, with all she's doing to lead Allen away from you, I see my fears were warranted."

"I got you. But, after seeing what Rhonda's done and knowing you worked with her, how are we to know you're not in on the scheme as well? I'm not trying to be rude, but I worry about my family, and outside influences aren't always the best when it comes to family affairs."

There it is, Sy thought. *Sally will never trust Patty as long as she's hanging with me.*

"I understand, but you need to realize, I'm worried for Allen the same as you are. He was a patient under my care, and I feel I've let him down. I need to atone for that and see Rhonda doesn't hurt anyone else."

Before Sally could respond, a car horn blared from outside.

"Tom's here. I'll give him the scoop on what's going on. He probably won't be happy about it, but he'll go along. I'll have him follow you out there."

Sally walked outside to talk to Tom while Sy and Patty got ready to leave. Sy quickly brushed his teeth and put deodorant on under a fresh shirt. Everything else stayed the same as the night before. He'd take a proper shower later.

When he opened the door to the bedroom, he saw Patty downing two small pills with a glass of water. The Ibuprofen he forgot to give her. She seemed resourceful enough and found everything okay. She dressed sensibly in capri pants and a v-neck top showing just the right amount of cleavage.

Sy felt like he was staring too much, so he had to look away. The fact was, he couldn't get the image from earlier—her half naked in his living room—out of his mind. Emotions he thought buried were coming back in waves. But, for now anyway, he had to get focused on the task at hand, helping Allen. Besides, the girl wasn't interested in his gender, so nothing to worry about.

"Could you drive again? If you don't mind? My head is still pounding. I should have listened to you last night. That home brew does have quite the kick," Patty said.

"I'll give you credit, you lasted longer than I thought you would. But yes, I'll drive."

She smiled and lifted her coffee mug for another sip.

"Hey, Sy?"

"Yeah."

"Thanks for taking up for me in front of your daughter. That took guts." She leaned in to give him a small kiss on the cheek.

Sy straightened at the suddenness of it, feeling a strange heat in his face. He turned away so she wouldn't see him blush. "No problem. You ready to go?"

"Lead the way," she said.

Chapter Twelve

A Visit to the Farm

Steam rose from the field by the Owens' farm as the sun boiled away the morning dew. Samson thought it produced a mystical quality. It promised to be a nice day. He stood stoically at the entrance of the tent, greeting the orange ball peaking over the horizon. Their night of hunting was over, and a new group of soldiers were ready to take their place among Rebecca's hive.

He would be responsible for them, as always. They would need guidance, as all young children. What to do; what not to do; to realize, even though you feel like it, you are not invulnerable to everything in the world. But for a little bit, he would enjoy the morning. He loved it, had for more than one hundred and fifty years.

His eyes wandered away from the sun and over to the old farmhouse sitting off the road. The farmer was outside milling around. Samson waved, but the old man paid no attention, continuing to walk aimlessly about the front lawn. Standing on the porch was the other half of the duo. His wife stared off into the horizon, seemingly unaware of why she was there.

Samson smiled, knowing Sage had charmed them into oblivion. The unkempt yard was looking poorly. No one had mowed it for the past couple of weeks. He figured the house inside was the same. Eventually, someone would come along and notice, but by then, Rebecca would have had her way with the town, and the parts would be ready for hibernation, feeding from Rebecca's energy.

Surprisingly, no neighbors had visited them other than the hillbilly from next door. Samson and Sage smelled him coming from a mile away.

The Pendleton's picked the right place for Rebecca to set up shop. A sleepy town with little to no police presence, and a mine full of workers to selectively feed from until the time was right to surface. It all seemed perfectly planned, but then he supposed it was. Once they were done, the boxes would be full again and they could invade the next town.

The Cadillac was hidden and would remain so for a while. It had been seen too many times over the previous couple of days. The local police would eventually call their state counterparts. Then, they would have to explain what they were doing, and of course, he would need to fix it. A wrinkle in the plan he didn't want to deal with. Better to stay hidden.

When the tent was first erected—Sage's idea—Samson figured they'd have many curious onlookers hanging around, but the opposite had happened. People paid little attention to it, partly due to Sage charming half the town with his magician shows and to the fact no one cared. Nothing was out of sorts about a traveling preacher coming to town. Sage had told Samson he'd grown up in a similar place and knew how to attract the people while blending into the background.

"Give them what they crave. Guidance," he had said.

So far, it was working. The missing piece was Allen. Rhonda found someone who grew up on the Salt Flat soil, one approved by Rebecca, and then practically pushed him into the sinkhole. Rebecca attached to his signature. A little careful planning and he was in a place where Rhonda could watch him incubate.

That is, until his father decided to break him out. But the plan still worked. Rhonda duped the family into letting her become his nurse. The power of desire was well embedded in her, and she used it to her advantage. The thing Samson couldn't understand, though, was why Rebecca wanted to make him a general as Samson and Sage were. Why couldn't he be an underling like Rhonda and Harley? He supposed Rebecca saw something in him Samson did not. Either way, he and the brothers would need to hibernate for one cycle before they could walk about, as he and Sage did shortly before the parts came back.

He was useful the night before, Allen and the brothers for that matter. People opened their doors for them, and once inside, it was easy to conceal the reason they were all there. The night's campaign was successful. Half the town was in the tent. The rest would come for the Revival, maybe others from neighboring towns as well. After Sage charmed them at the concert, they'd be begging to become part of the hive. Some would be worthy, but others would serve as food for the parts. It would be a glorious blood bath either way.

But they only had a short window to make it all work. The mixed parts would need to hibernate again after they fed, then Rebecca could be as powerful as she once was, ruling over the minions below her. He would be by her side, as always. She'd helped him when he was at his lowest, and he never forgot, pledging his undying loyalty to her forever those many years before in the dark streets of Baltimore. Puffing his inhaler, he thought about those times.

Samson remembered walking home as he did every night by the dimly lit lampposts, traveling by foot until he was on a road with nothing to light it at all. In those days, he lived a mile out of town where the street lighters didn't venture. He didn't worry, though. He was a big man with no family and had little to fear. And even though his lungs were scarred from tuberculosis at a young age, he could still handle himself well enough in a fight.

While at the pub where he worked, he'd helped a fellow out one night. His name was Poe, and he told many an interesting story in his drunken stupor. Even had a few stories published in the papers.

One night, the man had consumed so much he could barely stand up. Samson helped him out the door and attempted to find a carriage to take him home. Five good sized men followed. The men tried to rob them, but Samson intervened to even the odds. He fared well with all but two of the men still standing when the fight was over, and they weren't standing well.

The next night, in appreciation, Poe bought him a few drinks. Samson wasn't working that night, so he partook a bit too much, resulting in a stumbling walk home. This led to misjudgment on his part. The men he'd beaten up were waiting for him on the street outside his home, a few brandishing weapons. They numbered ten by then, too many for Samson to fight on his own.

In his condition, there was no denying he was a dead man, but it didn't mean he wouldn't go down fighting. He raised his fists, swung, and connected with the first man to advance on him. The man's jawbone cracked, and he crumbled like a rag doll.

Samson, swinging wildly in the dark, prepared for the next assailant, determined to hit someone. But to his surprise, no others advanced on him. With his drunken vision, he saw a man lifted into the air and consumed by the darkness. The unmistakable sound of bone crunching and flesh tearing could be heard in the woods. Screams like banshees permeated the trees, and Samson stepped back, looking around, waiting for something worse than his attackers to come out. What he saw surprised him.

A woman, as naked as the day she was born, walked from the shadows. Red liquid ran down her chin and onto her breasts. His pants tightened at the spectacle. Somehow, the blood aroused him as much as the nakedness of the girl.

She spoke the sweetest words in his ear. "Strong man, you will be my protector."

Her jaw extended downward, her face opening like a chasm. Teeth in rows sprouted from her gums, like that of a ravenous sea creature. Somewhere deep inside, Samson felt he should run, but something about the woman made him stay, his attraction too great to look away. She bit and ripped pieces of flesh from him. He felt pain, but nothing like he thought it should be. This pain was pleasurable, a wanting he couldn't understand, maybe wasn't meant to.

Consumed by thoughts of her, his mind became blank to everything else. He blacked out for a while and awoke on the trail, covered in blood. When he stood, he knew his life had changed forever.

Rebecca coaxed him toward her and pointed at a few of the men who lay beaten but not dead on the side of the road. He ate the men who tried to attack him and made them soldiers for Rebecca. They would later be among the others who stayed in the box until it was time to come out thirty years later.

Because of his strength, he was elevated above the rest, becoming a general, preparing her way each time she rose from the ground. He was the only one, too, until the day the Sage came along, charming Rebecca as much as she did him.

Samson never understood why Sage became her number one and he second. It had something to do with his family connections, a secret she never revealed. Because of her ties to Sage, the Pendleton Corporation rose from the ashes, a very useful group when they were needed.

But since she'd placed yet another as general, although it wasn't clear where he'd be in the hierarchy, the thought did occur to Samson where that would leave him. Even though it hurt, it didn't matter. He would do, as always, whatever his queen commanded.

Pulling into the road in front of the Owens' farm, Sy spotted a large sign on the side of the road in announcement of the event to come.

COME TO AN OLD-FASHIONED TENT REVIVAL
SEE THE WONDERS OF YESTERYEAR
AND MARVEL OVER THE MAGIC OF THE SAGE.
FRIDAY, JULY 9TH
MUSIC AND DANCING TO PRECEDE THE EVENT

Sy shook his head and wondered how crazy the dance would be. There hadn't been a street dance, or a tent revival for that matter, since he was a kid. Yet both were coming.

He pulled in the Owen's driveway with Sally and Tom behind him. He noticed Bob Owens right away, milling around the front yard, tending to the weeds growing around the sidewalk. The old man wasn't doing much of a job at it. They were overtaking everything.

Sy stepped out of the car and called to the farmer. "Hey, Bob! How's it going?"

Bob said nothing, only continued with the task at hand. Curiously, Sy watched Bob picked up a grasshopper from one of the tall blades of crabgrass. He considered it for a moment and then ate it.

Sy listened to the audible crunch of the farmers delicacy, and his stomach turned. When he saw the slime roll down Bob's chin, clear with black flecks, Sy ran to the side of the house and emptied the contents of his stomach. Patty followed him.

Sally exited the car, leaving Tom behind the steering wheel where he always stayed when they were out, the a/c on full blast. The July heat obviously made her uncomfortable. Beads of sweat formed on her forehead from the assault of the humid air. She saw Myrtle standing on the front porch and went to talk with her.

"Myrtle? How's the family doing?" The woman stared into the horizon, toward the hills, in the direction of the mine. Undeterred, Sally grabbed Myrtle by the arm and turned the woman toward her.

Myrtle looked right through her while she spoke. "Her wrath knows no boundaries. We'll all be redeemed in her blood, then live together as one."

"What kind of nonsense has this Sage put in your head? You go to the same church I do, and Reverend Mooney don't talk like that. You sound like a Catholic, always worshiping Mary."

Pulling away, Myrtle turned her head toward the horizon, looking into the rising sun, her eyes not flinching from the glare.

Sally descended the steps, walking quickly toward the car, but was stopped by Bob, who was blocking the sidewalk. Flecks of black and green covered his chin, and a slimy ooze crept from his mouth. He chewed on it like a cow would a cud. She stepped into the grass and ran to the car, her large breasts flopping in her shirt, threatening to hit her in the face if she didn't slow down. She yelled to Sy.

"We have to go now!"

He looked at her confused. "But, why? We just got here."

"I'm going for Sheriff Oeny, Dad. Somethings going on here, and I don't like it."

"We haven't even checked out the tent yet," Sy called back.

"Close the damn door, Sally. You're letting my air out," Tom yelled from inside the car.

"Well, you and your girlfriend can stay here. Me and Tom are leaving. I'll send the sheriff out. I don't think you should go anywhere near that tent."

The car backed out and drove to the road, turning toward town.

Patty watched as they left. "Well, looks like it's you and me now."

"I guess so. Want to check the tent out?"

"Sure, it's what we came here for," she said. "And to find Allen and Rhonda. You think they're in there?"

"Only one way to find out." Sy walked toward the entrance.

A strong wind picked up as they came within a few feet of the tent, colder than typical summer air. The canvas door flaps whipped furiously, creating a smacking noise as they hit the sides of the canvas structure.

Patty turned her head to shelter from the onslaught of dirt and dust flying toward her. As she did, she heard a whisper, sending a chill creeping up her back, a pleading voice from somewhere near the tent.

"Don't be fooled by her. Go now."

She saw a young girl, flicking in and out of existence, hauntingly staring at her. Strangely, it looked like she had a child in her arms.

Sy heard the whisper as well, training his gaze on the same area.

Patty and Sy simultaneously turned and ran towards the car.

"Did you see that?" Patty asked breathlessly.

"I saw my dead wife. She looked strange, like some black and white movie, a silent picture. I don't know what it was. I'm with Sally, though. We need more help. I don't know about the sheriff, but somebody.

Sy backed out of the driveway and roared towards the highway.

Samson stood just inside the doorway of the tent, watching all that transpired with fascination. He peered at the ghosts, their world open to his eyes.

"Ah, the dead are restless today. Will they be tomorrow? Who can tell? The barriers are falling. Soon, Rebecca will bridge the gap between the living and the dead, and all sins will be revealed."

Chapter Thirteen

Party Time

Tom wasn't paying much attention to the speed limit with Sally spurring him to go faster. He was irritated and ready to go home, just forget the whole thing. Fuck everyone in the town. If they wanted to go out there to the tent, then so be it. He wanted no part of it. If it weren't for Sally, he'd be out.

The people in the parking lot of Sam's Grocery all turned to see who was going so fast in a twenty-five-mile-per-hour zone, looking surprised to see it was one of their own upstanding citizens.

Sally instructed him to pull into the driveway of Sheriff Oeny's house. Tom watched as she hysterically exited the vehicle. Tom was glad the sheriff's car was there. It was much closer than the police station. The sheriff was walking out of his house as Sally ran to him.

"Ralph! Something bad is happening out at the Owens' farm. You got to come see. Myrtle didn't even say a word to me. How odd is that?"

Sheriff Oeny nodded to Tom in the car then regarded Sally. "It's not only there. Half the town is missing. Have you seen my wife? Greta should be here, but she's not and her car is parked in the garage. You think maybe she's gone out there to the tent?"

"I don't know, Ralph. I haven't seen her since the other day at the grocery. There's a lot of strange things going on around here. I don't know what to make of any of it."

"Well, I don't either. First my deputy, and now Greta."

"What happened to Bill?"

"He's dead, struck down in the line of duty."

"Oh my God. I'm sorry, Ralph. How'd he die?"

Ralph shook his head, his face troubled and ragged, like he hadn't slept in days. "I can't talk about it. The whole thing is still under investigation. If I were you, Sally, I'd stay away from that tent. Something bad's going on, and I don't want anybody I know messing around over there. I'm going to go over tonight after this street party and see if I can't get some answers. Right now, I have to get back to the station and make arrangements for Bill. If you see Greta, tell her I'm looking for her, could you?"

"Sure, Ralph. You look tired. I think you should get some sleep before going over there."

"I would if I could, but with the whole town falling apart and me being the one in charge, well, I can't. If this gets any wilder, I may have to call in the state police. I don't want to. The paperwork is a nightmare, but I'll do what I got to. You and Tom get home and wait on Eli. I hear they're letting school out early for this whole thing tonight. What the hell is going on around here?" Pulling his pants up, he got in his car, and backed out of the driveway, heading toward the station.

Sally got back in the car. "What's going on around here, Tom?"

Tom, giving his best reflection on the whole situation said, "Hell if I know."

After getting some breakfast over at the Mountain Perk—Patty's idea, as she liked the look of the place—they went back to his place to see if Allen and Rhonda had stopped by. As expected, no one was there. Once inside, they sat on the couch and turned on the television. It was only twelve, and they still had the better part of the day to kill before the street dance that evening.

Patty, obviously bored, looked at Sy. "You got any cards?"

"I'm sure I have a deck in the kitchen. What do you have in mind?"

"Well, I always played rummy while I was on vacation. You ever play?"

He thought back on all the time he and Sadie spent playing the same game and smiled. "Yeah, I play, and I'm damned good at it, so be warned."

Retrieving the cards, Sy shuffled the deck and dealt seven cards to each of them. They played for two hours. Sy, just as he told her, was an expert player, winning all but one game. Patty even voiced her suspicions that he let her win that one.

"Hey, Sy. You think it's too early to start on the hooch? You know, a little hair of the dog to end the nagging hangover."

"Hooch, huh? Is that what we're calling it now? Sure, knock yourself out. But I don't mean that literally."

"Don't worry, I'm still reeling from last night. I just need enough to take the headache away."

After Sy had poured two glasses, Patty lifted hers towards him. "To a wonderful new friendship."

Lifting his glass to meet hers, Sy said, "I'll drink to that."

Rhonda felt like weeping as she took in the spectacle before her. The parts, some swirling and others floating in the air high above the tent, paid homage to Rebecca, who was standing with her hands above her head on the stage. It brought a sense of pride to Rhonda. After all, she was responsible for many of them.

The previous sixty years brought many converts her way. Some she had to kill, but others, many others, were there, hovering above. The buzzing sound they made was pure ecstasy, and it overwhelmed her so much that she found herself horny and in need of bedding someone. Allen, or maybe one of the new boys. Maybe all of them. She didn't care, as long as someone met her needs. As she was pondering, she watched Jesse and Nathan separate and mix with the rest above. Well, any thought she had there was gone for the moment, but she noticed Allen wasn't with them.

She spotted him behind the stage, looking through a small slit in the side of the tent. She began to disrobe until the only article of clothing she had on was her shoes. Her hips swayed in a seductive manner, the sultry afternoon air invigorating to her midsection and breasts. She hugged him, grinding her womanhood on his leg.

"Take your clothes off, Allen. I've got a surprise for you."

He did as he was asked but didn't regard her advances, only continued to stare through the opening. Taking his member in her hand, she coaxed him to eagerness, then went to her knees to perform a seductive act of fellatio on him. After a minute, she realized she was getting no reaction. She stared at him, frustrated. He was still watching something outside.

"What the fuck, Allen? Doesn't this turn you on?"

"Yeah, I guess so. Rhonda? Don't you think it strange the dead walk around here?"

She rose to stand next to him and looked outside. Several apparitions floated aimlessly around the field, running through each other, through trees and other solid objects.

"No, not really. Every time Rebecca comes back, they do that. She's like a conduit for the dead or something. It's pretty strange but cool, too. Have you seen anyone you know?"

"A few. My great aunt Bessie walked through the car a minute ago. I thought I might have seen my mom, but I'm not sure."

"Have any talked to you?"

He looked at her strangely. "No. Do they do that?"

"Sometimes. I guess if they feel the need. It's always in a whisper, almost imperceptible, like it comes on the wind. Crazy."

"It is. Also, the way they look like old movie clips, flickering in and out, like they can't maintain focus. I've never seen anything like it. They all look the same, except the one I saw in the mine before my transformation. A blonde girl appeared to me, holding a baby. She was wounded and half the baby was missing. It was pretty creepy. I haven't seen her tonight though."

"She doesn't sound like any of the ghosts I've seen. Maybe it was just an image Rebecca produced for whatever reason. I don't know. I wouldn't worry too much about it though," she said glibly, realizing it must have been one of Allen's suppressed memories Sage spoke of.

"At first, I didn't, until I realized who it was." He looked at her with a troubled gaze, his brows furrowing.

"What do you mean?"

"It was, Nicole, Rhonda. It took me a lot of searching, but the memory of her was there, just below the surface. With Sage's help, I found it."

She looked at him inquisitively. "Sage helped you?"

"Yes. When he was in my head, he triggered the memory. It's why I think she appeared to me in the mine. She was trying to tell me something. I remember now. It was about the night she died. When she found out about us. I also remember the funeral, and how the casket was covered. Why? They only do that if someone is badly mutilated. Maybe because they were shot in the head. Maybe because of suicide. It makes sense to me. She killed herself because of us. When I saw her in the mine, she was holding a baby. Was she pregnant, and I didn't know?"

Rhonda turned her head, bit her lip, and then returned her gaze to him with a sigh. "Well, she did show up at an inopportune time. We were taking a shower together. I suppose it was bad, but she was weak. Nicole did kill herself and the baby, too. I wanted to tell you but didn't think it a good idea until you were ready. She was obviously messed up. You deserve better, Allen."

He angrily grabbed her by the wrist. "She had a tough upbringing. That much I do remember. Her daddy was hard on her, abused her, not only emotionally but physically, too. Maybe even sexually. I always suspected it was so, anyway. Nicole wanted out of this town more than I did. She was clinging to me for escape more than anything. I think she knew I didn't love her, but we were still friends. As long as I took her away from here, she didn't care about the rest. When you came along, I suppose I was looking for a way out. I would've left Nicole long before if I thought she could make it on her own."

She stared at him. "It's good your memory is coming back. I guessed as much. I'm good at reading people, Allen. I could tell you needed something more than you were getting. When Nicole died, I thought you'd come back here and leave me for good. I guess in some ways it was fortunate you fell in that sink hole and came to my hospital. Since

I got to care for you. I told myself if you ever got away again, I'd find you no matter what, and here we are."

Allen gazed into her eyes. "Did I tell you I think I was drawn to the sinkhole? I mean, I felt I was supposed to go there. Don't ask me why. My memories are coming back to me, but it's hard to piece that time together. The one of Nicole is new."

"I guess it's a good thing, then. Hopefully when you do piece it together, you'll see the memories of me are the best ones." She smiled and rubbed his member, changing the subject. "Hey, are you excited for the big party tonight? It all starts in a few hours."

"I guess so. I wonder how my family will feel, though. They're probably looking for me right now."

"Don't worry about them, Allen. We're your family now." Rhonda looked toward the stage. "Let's go talk to Rebecca. She'll sort all this out."

"Okay, I suppose," he said, tepidly.

Near the entrance of the tent, Nathan and Jesse McCarthy incorporated, bringing their body parts together, joining legs and arms to torsos. They seemed to be getting the hang of it, considering the short time they'd been converted.

Right before they joined the others, they'd found out Rebecca had plans for them. At least, Sage told them she did. They were instructed to go to Samson waiting outside with the car, the door open for them to enter. Sage had said he'd given Samson instructions to take the boys on a little errand. Once inside the car, Samson and the McCarthy boys headed out to the highway.

Sage stood in the shadow of the motor home, watching them speed away. The sun would be dipping behind the hills soon, and it would be full night, just in time for the revival. But first, he knew he must prepare for the street party. He would need to be ready for the show, wearing his preacher black and top hat to set things off.

The apparitions were gliding through the air around him. Their numbers seemed to be increasing, more than he'd ever seen before. The wind picked up, and he heard Sadie's voice in the distance.

"Damien, Damien, why do you do this?" the Sadie ghost said, then appeared in front of him suddenly. She was young and beautiful, with long blond hair and thin features, her eyes large and inviting, as blue as the ocean.

"Sadie? Is that you?"

"Yes, Damien. I'm appearing to you as my grandmother did, the way you remember her. I come to you, Damien, to plead you turn back. Leave this witch and be one with your family. Lay in rest forever, the natural way."

"I don't know what you're taking about., I'm fine with, Rebecca," he scoffed.

"No, Damien, you're lying to yourself. Reach deep within to remember who you are. Resist her. She is using your energy against you."

Sage shook his head, troubled by feelings he hadn't felt for a long time. He extended his hand toward her, but before he could grasp it, a hand ripped through the Sadie ghost, causing her to dissipate. It was Rebecca.

She gave Sage a disappointed look. "What are you doing? The ghosts will tell you all sorts of lies. I've told you this. You can't trust them, and never touch them. They could enter your body, even if you're my charge. Now, go. Be ready for the party tonight. It will be a good night for soul gathering."

Sage had no words for her, only turned for the motor home once again. But before he entered, he looked toward the apparitions again to see if he spotted Sadie. There was no sign of her, but he was sure it wouldn't be the last time he'd see her, no matter what Rebecca said.

Henry McCarthy pulled into the driveway leading up to his home, just back from talking to Sheriff Oeny, something about his boys being implemented in the death of somebody. Jess and Nathan were hard asses, the way he taught them to be, but they wouldn't kill anyone. But then again, he hadn't seen either one of them since the evening before when they went to the bar. The sheriff said that's where the shit went down. He also said he saw Jesse's truck in the parking lot. Another strange occurrence, as Jesse worshiped his custom Chevy and wouldn't just abandon it. Henry didn't know quite what to make of the whole situation.

As he got closer to the house, the bright sun glared in his face, making it hard to see. He squinted and pulled in by the barn. The light was blocked by the building, casting a shadow on the house, increasing the visibility. He noticed the front door was half-opened.

He put the truck in park and got out. Ole Shep usually greeted him, but with the door being open, he wondered if his prize German Shepherd wasn't running free. He couldn't see it, though. Shep would protect the house and Henry with the last breath of his life. But there was no barking anywhere. The house was eerily quiet.

"Who's here?"

No answer. He reached in the truck and retrieved the 30.06 rifle from the rack in the back window. He pulled back the bolt and slipped a shell in the chamber, then eased up to the front porch of the house. The steps creaked under his weight, but he kept going, holding his rifle in front of him. Henry put the barrel against the door and pushed it open the rest of the way, nervously aiming the rifle, swinging it side to side. He was ready to shoot anything coming at him.

He was about to lower it when he heard a voice close by.

"Hey, daddy. What 's you up to with that gun?"

"Jesse? That you?"

"It's me. I was wondering when you would get home."

"Where have you been, son? Where's your brother?"

"Right here, Daddy," Nathan said from the other side of the room.

"I was worried about you boys. The sheriff called; said you'd all been in a fight with the Sutton boy. Said there was lots of blood."

Even though it was still light outside, the living room lay cast in shadow. Henry, wanting to get a better look at the boys, reached behind him for the light switch on the wall.

"You can leave it off. I can see you just fine; read you, too. Your mind is an open book, full of all the bad things you've done," Jesse said.

Henry lowered his arm from the wall. "What do you mean?"

"Nicole, Daddy. The things you did to her drove her right to the grave. We blamed Allen, but after reading your thoughts, we can see what you really did."

"I-I don't know what you're talking about. Your sister's dead, for God's sake. I had nothing to do with it."

Nathan's mouth formed a devious grin. "Now, daddy, don't try to get one over on us. We know."

"It's okay, though. We can forgive you," Jesse added.

"Boys, you're scaring me. You need to stop." Henry held the gun in front of him, the barrel trembling.

"Do you think that will stop us? She has shown us the way. Rebecca is coming soon, and then all will know the meaning of true life. Daddy, you have sinned and must be shown the way to repent, with blood."

"Boys, we can talk about this. I need to see you in the light, make sure you're okay." Henry reached for the light switch again. This time he found it. The room lit up, and his eyes widened at what he saw.

Shep lay in pieces across the white carpeted floor, his head perched in front of Henry, tongue laying to the side. Blood soaked the light-colored carpet, producing a trail leading to Jesse, who was sitting naked on the couch. The pallid color of his skin and dark eyes void of any color looked stark against the dark brown faux leather. Blue veins pulsed over his body. His mouth was covered in blood, dripping down his chin and onto his chest. Nathan sat close by in the matching recliner; his features almost identical to Jesse's.

"Sorry about Ole Shep. I didn't want to hurt him, but I guess he didn't recognize us anymore."

"What the hell happened to you boys? Let me call the sheriff and get you some help." Henry stepped backward toward the door. He tried to get a bead on his sons, or whatever they were, but couldn't steady his hand, the gun barrel shaking up and down.

The McCarthy boys, blood-stained and ravenous, approached Henry.

"Stay back, boys. I said stay back!"

The gun blast echoed through the house, along with Henry's scream.

Rhonda led Allen to the stage and bowed before Rebecca. She stepped aside, allowing Allen to stand before her.

"Allen, my new general. How are you feeling?" Rebecca said.

"Well, this new power within me is intoxicating."

"Good. It should be." She probed deeper, her mind connecting with his. "I see something troubles you."

"Yes, my queen. I have memories coming back to me, things from my previous life."

"This is to be expected. All things will be revealed, and in proper sequence once you've completed a cycle of hibernation with me."

"I suppose."

He felt her consuming his mind. The girl he thought was Nicole, the glimmer of her, like some reflection from a pool of water, began to fade, replaced by Rebecca. He tried to resist, but she held on, gripping tighter to his thoughts until he was unable to keep her from them.

"Good. You are strong, everything I would expect the mind of one such as yourself to be. You come from a family of very powerful people. You, as Sage has, will rise to a place of higher elevation in my collective. Rhonda?"

Rhonda smiled and knelt next to Rebecca. Rebecca stroked her long, red hair lovingly, like a mother would her child.

"See to his every need. Make him as happy as you can."

"Yes, my queen, with pleasure." Rhonda reached for Allen, pulling him close to her in a loving embrace, grinding her hips to him.

Rebecca smiled as the two made their exit from the stage.

Rhonda led Allen to an area in back of the tent. She bent forward and touched her toes, swaying her hips in a come-get-me motion. Allen responded in kind, entering her with a renewed fervor. The two moved with each other, Allen thrusting and Rhonda pushing herself against him, until they both groaned from the climax of the orgasms.

After she settled down, Rhonda, still as horny as she was before, looked at Allen. "You ready for round two?"

She stroked him to erection again, but before he could respond, he noticed something near the edge of the stage. It was Nicole. She stood there, a jumbled mix of sepia tones and color imagery flickering frantically in and out of reality. The wound to the right side of her head as prominent as ever. His eyes were drawn to the area, realizing this is where she shot herself. Allen trained his eyes on her lips as she mouthed words to him.

Rhonda, noticing he'd become a limp noodle in her hands, became increasingly frustrated. She didn't care what Rebecca said, she needed more than what she was getting from Allen. Maybe she'd find the McCarthy boys after all, take them both on, as her mood suited such things. No matter who it was, they'd be happy they engaged.

"Be seeing you, Allen." She left him standing there alone.

He barely noticed. His eyes studied Nicole, trying to read her lips. He felt her tugging at his thoughts and relaxed, letting the words fill his mind.

"She seeks to destroy the womb, but the child lives on."

She repeated the phrase over and over. Allen closed his eyes and dropped to his knees as he felt her enter his body and his mind. The world around him faded away. When he opened his eyes, he was standing in the bathroom of his home in Lexington, watching Nicole standing in only her panties, rubbing her belly in front of a mirror. She looked every bit the beauty he remembered from his youth, glowing in a way he hadn't seen before. Her stomach was swollen. Apparently, the recent weight gain she'd been complaining about was only a cover for something else.

He stepped forward, wanting to go to her and embrace his wife, but he realized he couldn't move. He was only an observer, unable to influence anything.

He saw Rhonda standing outside the bathroom door with a pistol in her hand, slowly easing her way into the room. A struggle ensued, leaving Rhonda holding Nicole by the hair, the gun pushed under her chin.

"I'd bring you into the collective if it wasn't for Allen. I'm afraid there's only room for one woman in his life, and she doesn't care for children." Rhonda pulled the trigger.

Blood and brain matter splattered the wall as the bullet exited through Nicole's right eye. Rhonda eased his wife's limp body onto the toilet, placing the gun in her blood-drenched hand to make it look like she'd killed herself, then left as quickly as possible.

Allen woke suddenly. He was enraged, ready to find Rhonda and get an explanation. He was surprised, though, to see Rebecca standing before him, her olive-colored skin radiant in the hazy afternoon light shining through the thin walls of the tent, almost angelic in presence.

"I see Rhonda has disregarded my request. She will be dealt with. It may be time for a cleansing of my ranks." She coaxed him to stand and looked into his eyes. "Pay no attention to what the ghosts are telling you. They deceive even the best of my generals. Come to me."

She touched her hands to his forehead, and Allen felt her presence throughout him. His mind and body took in all of her. He found himself forgetting what he was doing. Rebecca was who he lived for, breathed for, fought for. She encompassed his whole being. He would do anything for her. She led him from the tent, guiding the newly charmed Allen to the motor home. The door opened, and Sage, waiting as if he expected them, guided Allen in to have a seat.

"Take good care of him, Sage. He has much to do." Rebecca then returned to the tent.

Rhonda's desires clearly clouded her ability to do her job. Rebecca found her cavorting with three men, all recent converts, back at the tent and felt it time to end those distractions. All her gains from the past one hundred years would be for nothing if she couldn't keep her generals in line. Sage and Samson understood that better than the rest, but Rhonda and Allen were still too young to get a full grasp on the direness of the situation at hand. Everything could be lost so easily. Rebecca had to take hold of the situation.

She flew to the top of the tent and stopped a few feet from Rhonda. The girl was in the throes of ecstasy as Rebecca entered her mind with a thunderous shout. "Do you forget who you are?"

Rhonda threw the men from her. They separated to join the other swarming parts.

"My queen, I'm sorry, I was only relaxing a little, getting ready for tonight," she said nervously.

"Well, because of your absence, your charge now knows what you were hiding from him. A ghost was able to enter his mind and plant the seed there. I've charmed him so he'd forget, but now the memory is there and will eventually come out." Rebecca's voice dripped with disdain.

"Does he know I killed Nicole? Surely he doesn't."

"Yes, he knows, and if I hadn't intervened, he would have found you." Rebecca turned from Rhonda, the hurt evident in her voice. "I should have let him."

"I'm sorry, my queen. I'll do better. Where is he now?"

Rebecca raised her head and breathed in, then faced Rhonda. "He's safe with Sage at the moment. You've done enough for now. Get your head straight. This gathering is more important than you know. It's nothing like the last in your small town, the one I plucked you from to become a new general in my ranks. This one will test the loyalty of all my people. There are forces gathering here. I feel they mean to do us harm."

Rhonda lowered her head. Rebecca saw in her mind how she remembered what those times were like, the gutter she'd found Rhonda in, the needle stuck in her arm. It was a memory she was sure the girl would rather forget.

Rebecca looked at her and smiled. "Good. Keep those thoughts close by you the next time you decide to disobey me. I can send you back anytime, to a bottom worse than the one you came from, one where the worms won't regard your dead and bloated body. Now, get ready for the party. You will help Allen with what he needs. His family will become part of the collective, and he can end his loyalty to them. He must be mine and mine alone if we are to complete the cycle."

Rhonda nodded, lowering herself to the floor below and walking out of the tent. Rebecca watched as the parts swarmed busily in a circle, responding to her close proximity.

"Yes, my children, I'm here and you have nothing to worry about. Feed me, and I'll feed you."

The parts buzzed, excited by the proclamation of their queen.

Chapter Fourteen

Tent Revival

Patty and Sy were on their second jar of shine and had played enough cards. They both figured it was about time to start getting ready for the street party. Hopes of seeing Allen and Rhonda there was the only motivator for going at this point.

"You want some more?" she said, shaking the jar at Sy.

"I probably shouldn't if I'm going to drive to the party."

"Suit yourself." She poured a glass. "I think I have to pee. Be right back." Patty stood and tilted backward.

Sy caught her before she fell into the coffee table. "Whoa, I think you've had enough," he said.

"I'm forty-five -years -old, and I think I know when I've had enough, buddy." She put a finger in the middle of his chest.

When she returned from the bathroom, her gait was that of many a patron leaving the bar at closing time. She paid little attention to where her feet were being placed, tripped over the couch, and fell into the waiting arms of Sy.

Realizing where she was, she said, "Let's dance."

Sy knew she was drunk and would probably regret what she was doing later, but he did want to dance with her. What the hell. How often did he get the chance to do such a thing anyway? He led her to the kitchen and turned the radio on to the local country station playing a decent dancing tune, something with a honkytonk beat.

After the song had ended, he led her toward the couch. Sy figured she'd sit there for a moment while he made coffee. But instead of letting go of Sy, she pulled him toward her. He lost his balance and fell into her as she extended her arms and legs around him, pulling him even closer. He tried to release himself from her, but she insisted.

She looked at him with lazy eyes. "Don't you know when a girl is flirting with you?"

"I thought you liked girls?"

"I do, but I also like guys. I'm much more discerning with that gender, though. I've discerned you're all right, Sy." She kissed him full on the lips.

He figured it was probably better to not allow it to go any further but wanted it to just the same. Sy gave in and returned the kiss. Their arms began to explore each other's bodies, and Sy felt pressure in his pants in an area he thought no longer responded. He was glad to see that wasn't the case.

He lightly groped on Patty's breasts. He figured they were a bit smaller than Sadie's, but when he realized he was thinking of his dead wife, guilt began to creep in. As Patty pulled her shirt off and unsnapped her bra, the thoughts faded.

The midsection pressure was increasing, and he felt the urge to get his pants off in a hurry. Once he pulled them off, she immediately released his member from his underwear. To his amazement and overall happiness, it stood proud and ready to serve. She pulled off her pants and panties, straddled him, and then guided him toward the sweet spot.

Suddenly, guilt flooded into his mind again. *This is happening, but I can't. What would Sadie think?*

"Wait, wait," Sy said, as he tried to pull away.

Patty stopped her advance. "What's wrong?"

"I'm sorry, it's been a while since I've done this, and never with anyone else except Sadie for the last thirty years. Don't get me wrong. I want to, but just take it a little slower with me. That okay?"

"Yes, it's fine, sweet actually." She kissed him on the nose. "It's been a while since I was with a man, so don't worry."

Slowly, she eased onto him, moving up and down in a rhythmic fashion. Patty seemed to want to do all the work, and he was grateful. To say he was rusty was an understatement. The whole act lasted three minutes with both groaning as they climaxed. They continued kissing for a few minutes as they lay naked against each other.

He seemed to be developing an affinity for the girl. Hard to believe they were at odds when they first met. The old phrase 'keep your enemies closer' took on a new meaning. He supposed it was official. He did have a girlfriend.

The stage was set next to the hill at the end of the IGA parking lot. Two subdivisions were above the store, and they were sure to hear the noise below. Large stacks of amplifiers were raised next to the platform to enhance the music of the band. Possum Spit, who played for the patrons of Pa-Rudy's bar, were making their debut in Salt Flat thanks to Allen Sutton and Rhonda Lane procuring them for the night's festivities. Allen and Rhonda themselves would be working the crowd, making way for Rebecca and Sage. The night promised to be a good one.

"Allen? You ready for tonight, your big debut?" Sage asked.

"Yes, I am," he said with enthusiasm.

"Good. This will be a night to shine. Show business, like religion, is all about the people. If they're on your side, anything is possible."

Sage patted Allen on the back and walked behind the stage where his motor home was parked. Those words were the gospel. His mentor spoke them to him, the words of the preacher, his father, the man who destroyed Damien Reynolds then built him back up, producing in him the ability to be the Sage.

He stopped on the first step of the motor home when he saw Jesse waving to him.

"Is the stage in the right place, Sage?"

"Yes. It's perfect. And what about your father? Did he come around?"

"Daddy's taken care of."

"Good. Now it's up to Allen to bring his family into the fold. I want no one getting in the way of what we're doing. This whole town will be ours before the night is through."

Yes, the stage was perfect, looking the way it did every time he put on this charade. The town, as Damien Reynold's town did, would fall to Allen Sutton who would become a general in Rebecca's hive. The young man seemed insignificant to Sage. He'd probably end up being a number three to her, which meant little in the hierarchy of things. But more hands to help would always be appreciated.

Once inside the motor home, Sage dressed in his preacher outfit. He checked himself in the mirror attached to the flimsy door and placed a top hat on his head. The hat made a nice touch, giving him a much more entertaining look than most holy men. Another trick his father taught him.

His father owned the hat at one time. Sage remembered taking it from his blood-soaked head. The man had big aspirations, even with

Rebecca, but it didn't turn out the way he wanted. Always ambitious, his father wanted to lead. He owned what would later become the Pendleton Corporation. Just a mining operation barely staying afloat when Rebecca found it. His only mistake was defying her, and ultimately bringing his demise. In the end, it was Sage who the preacher would look up to, Sage who took his spot by his queen, and Sage who turned the Pendleton Corporation into what it would become. How long had it been? Maybe a hundred years ago? Time was something he paid little attention to anymore. The show was what mattered, and the show would and must go on. Rebecca demanded it.

As he sat back in one of the recliner chairs, relaxing for a moment before his performance, he felt the air get colder. Someone, or something, was there with him. Sadie appeared in her full color version again. She said nothing, only stretched her hand to him. Hesitantly, he reached for her.

The frigid hand extended into his, melding together, becoming warmer as the ghost entered his body. For a moment, he remembered what Rebecca said about the ghosts, but as he felt the welcoming embrace of his granddaughter, all fear subsided.

His mind faded to a different time. He was coming home. A doughboy by the name of Damien Reynolds from the Great War. He'd seen his share of tragedy and wanted no more, only to live a peaceful life and settle down with his wife, although he knew it wasn't meant to be. He'd received a message after he got back to the states that she'd died in childbirth. Their daughter was staying with his brother and his wife. Although a hundred years before, those memories still seemed so fresh.

But then the scene changed, and he was seeing his daddy, holding an infant. His daddy took the blanket from the baby, and he could see it was a girl. She cried as she was laid on an altar of some kind. It was the one in front of the old church his daddy preached in. A woman stepped into the picture. Although fuzzy, Sage could see Rebecca as she reached for the child. But before she could claim it, his daddy pulled the infant away.

Rebecca fumed with anger as he ran to the back of the church. Sage saw as the tentacles grabbed hold of him and how the child was passed to someone just before he was killed. Another woman. Sage believed it to be his mother. She took the child and ran from the church. The memory faded, but as it did, he saw a cloud bank and Sadie standing there.

"Do you see it, Damien? It was your daughter they saved. Rebecca wanted to kill her to end our bloodline. Our people own a certain magic given to them long ago. We can destroy the parts and ultimately her. The ghosts who are gathering are part of your family. Rebecca knows this. It's why she's here, why the Pendleton's are helping her. They need her to prosper. The only way is to stop us. She seeks to destroy the womb so she can destroy the child, but the child lives on. Your child lived even though your wife died, not in childbirth as she would have you believe but by her hand. Your daddy found this out and thought he knew a way to stop her by using the caul from your daughter's amniotic sack. But it didn't work, and she nearly killed your daughter. With his help, though, she escaped, but he lost his life in the process. Once he died, she took you instead, knowing someday she'd gather enough strength to come back here and ultimately end the only thing that can stop her. She's used you all these years to get what she really wants, her immortality. If Allen brings his family into the collective, she will own the bloodline, and even the ghosts can't defeat her then. There would be no need to hibernate. She would be all powerful. As long as one of your family survives, she'll never stop."

She vanished for a moment, and Sage saw the head he took the hat from, the one from his father, the preacher who betrayed him. All that time. Could it have been the other way around? Confusion clouded his mind as she formed again in front of him.

"Damien, Rebecca has owned you for far too long. It's time to end it."

"But how is this possible? My daddy was a snake in the grass, always thinking of himself. He didn't care about my daughter."

"These are the things she wants you to believe. You knew the truth long ago. Search your heart, what's left of it, and you'll see. Mind you though, the ghosts of your family are gathering to defeat her, and we'll bring others. But we need you to invoke the name of Calypso."

Sage thought back on the day he'd lost Damien Reynolds and took his namesake. He and Samson had just defeated Calypso for Rebecca. He was nearly destroyed in the process.

"You want me to bring back the old witch who nearly killed me?"

"I know it sounds strange, but if we are to gather and defeat her, Calypso will need to be part of it. I can't do it. It has to be the one who banished her. You, Damien. You will need to choose a side very soon. Choose well."

Sage woke to a knock on the door. His dazed eyes focused on the large form of Samson standing there.

"It's showtime, Sage." He looked at the half-opened eyes of his friend. "Have you been sleeping?"

"A little. Sometimes it's good to rest before a big show."

"We can rest when we go back in the boxes. For now, we need to be on guard and ready for the bigger show tonight."

"Yes, I suppose you're right. Samson? Did you remember my daddy?"

"The preacher? Yes, I remember him. Don't you? You took his hat the day he died."

"I do recall doing so but don't remember why."

"He betrayed our queen and needed to be stopped. It's why she chose you instead. You were stronger than you father."

Sage smiled at the big man. "Thank you, my friend."

"No problem. I'll see you on stage," Samson said, then left through the door.

Sage walked to the mirror again. He tipped the hat forward a bit, then readjusted it. Sadie's voice still echoed in his mind.

Choose a side.

Should he? It wasn't the time to think about it; it was time for the show. He had to go.

Sally called Sy and arranged to meet up at the street party. This time he remembered to grab his cell phone from the nightstand. Patty, with the help of a few cups of coffee, had sobered enough to walk steady. She was still affectionate to Sy, something pleasing to him. Hopefully, she really did like him, and it wasn't just sex between them. Sy took those commitments seriously. He wouldn't give himself up to just anyone.

They could see Sam's place buzzing with excitement. A country music band was playing, and people were already dancing. Sally waited with Sy and Patty while Tom parked the car. Eli, who had decided to come, too, was with her. Most of his friends from school were there after all. He left, making his way through the large group of people gathered close to the store.

Once Tom caught up with them, they made their way across the highway and to the IGA parking lot. Sy directed Patty's gaze to the door of the grocery store where Sam was trying but failing to keep his store from being overrun by teenagers. He'd stop one group while another snuck behind him and into the store. As Patty laughed, Sy held her hand, squeezing it affectionately. It didn't go unnoticed by Sally, and he heard her whispering to Tom.

"Look at them. They think they're teenagers or something. I don't like it at all."

"Oh, come on, Sally. Your dad has to move on sometime. He don't want to be lonely forever," Tom replied.

"Well, I guess I'll have to get used to it, but I still don't like it. She's younger than him. What if she breaks his heart? Besides, she told me she liked girls."

"Seems she may have changed her mind, Sally. They look pretty chummy."

####

Eli pushed through the crowd, stopping when he saw a familiar face.

"Uncle, Allen? What are you doing here? Grandpa's been looking everywhere for you."

Allen scanned the crowd. "Where are they then?"

"Over by the edge of the parking lot," Eli said, pointing in the direction he'd seen his family last.

"Thank you, Eli. I'll talk to you later."

Allen waved at Rhonda, motioning for her to meet him at the edge of the crowd.

"My family is over there. Maybe it's time to welcome them into the flock?"

"My pleasure. Let's go."

The band was getting louder, and some boot scootin' boogie blared out to get the people in front, mostly the kids, to dance. The adults mingled in back, away from the offensive noise, passing a few cold ones around, courtesy of the coolers in back of their trucks.

Sy knew most of them and began introducing his friends to Patty. It'd been a while since Sy felt the way he did. In a word, he was happy. He'd been cooped up in his house for so long that he'd forgotten how to interact with people. The big fireworks display the week before didn't even bring him out, but there he was. He just needed the proper motivation, and Patty was it.

Buck and his family had been the only people Sy hung out with the past couple of years. There were others he hadn't seen for a long time, so long he forgot how much of a social bug he was when Sadie was alive. Many of his neighbors and fellow church goers were asking him questions, and no one seemed to act funny that he had a new girl on his arm. So enthralled he was in his rediscovered popularity that he failed to notice the hand on his shoulder until he was jerked around to face the man behind him.

"Allen? Is it really you?"

The Allen Sy remembered from a few days before was rail thin, sickly. Even when he woke, he hadn't regained his vigor, but he looked as though he'd been reborn into a new man, muscled and strong, full of color and vitality.

"Hey, dad. Miss me?" Allen picked Sy off his feet, holding to the collar of his shirt.

Sy reached for Allen's arms, clawing for release. He attempted to pull from his son's vice-like grip but couldn't, only struggled instead, his feet on tiptoes. The crowd stepped back, gasping at the sight of Allen holding Sy in the air.

Rhonda noticed the crowd's response to what was going on. "Allen? Maybe we should be more discreet."

At her urging, Allen lowered Sy to his feet.

Sy stepped away, his hands and legs shaking. He tried to regain his composure and straightened out his shirt and jacket.

"Nice to see you too, son. I was thinking you skipped town or something."

"He's been safe with me the whole time," Rhonda said.

Patty stepped toward Rhonda. "You, bitch. What have you done to him? I doubt Allen would ever do anything like that to his dad if you hadn't been involved."

Rhonda gazed curiously at Patty. "Patty? What are you doing here?"

"Looking for you, obviously. I figured you were up to no good, and now I know I was right. Keep your hands off Sy's family."

"Allen makes his own decisions. He's seen the light. Maybe you should, too. Besides, why does it matter to you? If I remember correctly, you and Sy weren't the best of friends."

Sy grasped Patty's hand and smiled at Rhonda. "Well, some things have changed. I see you were nothing more than a wolf in sheep's clothing. You were supposed to take care of my boy, not turn him against me. This lady has been a much better friend to me."

"Oh my God, no, Sy. I can't believe you'd have anything to do with Patty. She's such a control freak. Don't you see it?"

Sally, who'd been standing close by, stepped between the two. "Listen, you were supposed to take care of Allen and keep him home to recover properly, but all he's done is run the roads with you since he's gotten any semblance of health. It can't be good for him. He needs rest and his family. I'm firing you."

"Firing me? You don't know who you're talking to. You're as insignificant as an ant to me. Maybe you need to learn some manners." Rhonda lifted her hand, but before she could strike, Allen caught it.

"Don't worry, Sally. I can assure you, I'm in good shape now. Come on, Rhonda. I think it's time to go. Maybe the party needs to get going a little while. They'll come around once the Sage takes the stage."

Rhonda agreed. They turned and headed for the stage.

"What on earth was that about?" Sally said.

"I don't know. It seems like Allen is getting tied up with her in a bad way. I'm wondering now if it was a good idea bringing him home." Sy said.

Returning from his trip to the store, Tom looked over the exasperated expressions of Sally and Sy with a look of concern. "What happened? Was that Allen I just saw?"

"Yes. The girl he's with seems to be running the show for him at the moment. I don't know what to think. I fired her from taking care of him, but I don't think it will do any good. She's got her hooks in him and he's not coming around."

The band stopped playing suddenly, and the crowd grew silent. A lanky man, tall but good looking, took the stage. He wore a black suit with a white clerical collar. His sleeves were rolled up and buttoned at the elbows, no jacket, only a pinstripe vest suited for going under one. The strangest thing of the whole ensemble was the top hat he wore. Holding his hands above his head, he addressed the crowd with a commanding voice.

"Hello, Salt Flat! We're glad you all made it out to the party. Can we get a round of applause for the band?"

He stepped to the side and let everyone see the members of Possum Spit taking a bow. The crowd erupted with applause. Sage turned to them again and waved his hands, shooting fireworks over the cheering people. Near the edge of the crowd, children oohed and awed at the display.

"I'm glad you enjoy the magic, but I think we're really here to hear the word of God. Be prepared for the greatest delivery of the gospel you'll ever encounter. My magic comes from a higher power than me, and you'll get a taste of it and more during the revival!"

The eyes of the crowd widened, and they no longer laughed or cheered but swayed, knees weak, some falling where they stood. Part clergy man and part magician, Sage seemed to embody all of them, and the crowd, getting into the rhythm with him, seemed to be soaking in every ounce of what he was selling. However, Sy and Patty, along with Sally and Tom, weren't buying it at all.

Sage stepped to the side and Rebecca, coming from behind him, took center stage. Dressed in a sheer, nearly non-existent robe, she smiled at the crowd. She waved her arms in circles and spoke in a strange language they didn't understand, but then, the words suddenly became clear.

"My people, follow me. Go to the tent tonight. Go now. The line will be long. Wait patiently for your queen."

Sage and Rebecca watched the people surround the parking lot, heading for their cars. Rebecca relaxed, pleased with her work. But, as they watched, they noticed something disturbing.

Ghosts began filtering in behind the crowd, heading for the stage, a large number of them, more than they had seen in years.

Sage hesitated and eased for the edge of the stage.

The ghosts continued forward. Rebecca frowned and stepped backward, away from the oncoming invasion. "Sage? Help me."

But Sage wasn't there. He was exiting the stage, mingling in with the band members as they were leaving.

"What are you doing?" she cried to him.

He said nothing, only continued to go. Her voice now became thunder in his mind.

Tell me you aren't betraying me. Sage talk to me!

Sage hid in the shadows beside the stage, watching the ghosts advance on Rebecca.

She backed away slowly as the apparitions were getting closer. Hundreds of them weaved in and out of reality, flickering the way they always did, but instead of aimlessly milling about, they seemed to have purpose. All united in one common goal, to get to her.

Rebecca held her hands in front of her and muttered an ancient text from a language long dead. The ghosts stopped at the edge of the stage, unable to move past the invisible barrier she'd created. She turned and saw Samson—her strong man always—motioning her toward him. The Cadillac was parked beside the stage, already running and ready to go.

"The spell I placed won't last long. We need to get back to the tent, to my children, where I'm strongest. Take me there, Samson."

Samson helped her in and then took his place as driver. They saw the line of cars starting for the tent and were pleased. Even if the spirits were gathering, they would have no power once all those people were under Rebecca's umbrella.

Although they found it strange the dead were building in numbers, he thought it stranger when they saw that Sage had taken the motor home back without Samson's escort. They were supposed to lead the crowd in a glorious parade procession to the tent. Something was up with him, and Rebecca didn't like it.

Sy, feeling lightheaded, looked at Patty as she stumbled toward him. He caught her before she fell to the ground but lost his balance, dipped sideways and caught himself before he wiped out with Patty in his arms.

He saw something he couldn't quite comprehend. It was the thing he saw by the tent. Sadie, or it looked like her anyway, her figure, black and white, flickering furiously, saying something. It was almost a whisper. He could read her lips more than hear her.

She was pointing to his ears, then put her hand on hers. He understood she was telling him to cover his ears. He followed her directions and instantly began to get his composure. Sadie faded as soon as he did.

He released Patty from his arms, then guiding her to do the same with her hands, he stood and looked around at the crowd. They were all heading to their cars, including Sally and Tom with Eli in tow. Sy wanted to redirect them, but they were too far away, and he couldn't get their attention. The strange Egyptian-looking lady was on stage, waving her arms around. They seemed to be disconnected with her body, almost an illusion Sy supposed. But then, he had just seen his dead wife instructing him, so reality didn't seem to be working.

He kept his hands over his ears and nodded to where the car was parked. Halfway across the parking lot, Sy turned to see his son coming for him. Patty was ahead of him and heading for the car. He yelled a muffled warning, but it was too late. Rhonda had flanked them all and stood in Patty's path.

Sy had a feeling it wouldn't end well. He couldn't release his hands from his ears, so what chance did he have against his son? Especially as strong as Allen had become. Hell, Sy had a hard time with Allen when he was in his weakened condition only a couple of days before.

"Going somewhere, Dad?"

Sy heard a muffled version of what Allen was saying, more reading his lips than anything, but he understood fully what was implied. Sy tried to sidestep his son. No good. Allen lifted him into the air with one hand, and as Sy watched with horror, the other arm released from his body. It flew above Sy, awaiting further instructions. Sy felt he was seeing another illusion, but it seemed too real. Something had happened to Allen. It was all was too crazy.

The separated hand hovered then rose. It fell, picking up speed, coming straight for Sy. He was helpless to do anything other than struggle to get free. Just before the appendage hit him, though, it stopped, floating in mid-air in front of Sy. He slowly felt Allen releasing him.

"Dad? What's happening? Where am I?"

Sy saw Sadie with her hand on Allen's shoulder, keeping him at bay. Tiny tendrils of smoke rose from where she made contact with him. Sadie was giving him an opportunity to escape. He could see it, but would it last? Sy didn't stick around to find out.

Sy turned toward Patty. She looked at Rhonda, who had the same dazed expression as Allen did. A ghost stood behind Rhonda as well, one Sy recognized. It looked like Nicole, but there was no time to figure it out.

Sy seized his opportunity, grabbing Patty by the arm and guiding her to the car. Once inside, he fired it up and sped out of the parking lot in the opposite direction of the large convoy of cars headed to the tent.

Unable to move, Allen watched as his dad drove off. He tried to focus, but his head still buzzed. He looked to Rhonda for guidance, but she only stood there, trapped in the same half-dazed stupor.

Allen saw a ghost, no two of them, considering him from a few feet away. They appeared kind of jerky, as though the celluloid was worn and old. He recognized them both. One was his mom. She looked as radiant as when she was younger, as he remembered her in his childhood. The other ghost was Nicole. She looked at him, then faded away. His mom stayed for a moment, speaking to him quietly, like a whisper on the wind.

"Allen, come back to me. Remember who you are. Remember we're your family."

As she faded away, Allen watched her, his mind reeling with confusion. He looked to Rhonda, who was walking toward him. "What happened?"

"Hell if I know. One minute I was ready to grab the bitch, and the next I couldn't move, like I was caught in a fly trap or something. My shoulder feels like it's on fire. How about you?"

"Pretty much the same," he said, not saying anything about recognizing his mom.

"I felt the same thing in the mine when the ghost touched me. I don't know why, all of a sudden, they're doing that. Whatever's going on, it doesn't matter. We need to get back to the tent. I have a feeling those two will be there soon enough." She pointed toward Sy's car. "If we can't get them, there'll be a host of others who can. Let's go, Allen."

He scanned the empty parking lot, the stage the only thing there, and shook his head. Suddenly, he felt a deep longing for his childhood, his mom in particular.

Chapter Fifteen

Rebecca Rising

Henry McCarthy knew a few things. He knew his farm wouldn't work itself, and if he were to get any kind of harvest from the scrub of ground he owned, it would take him and his boys to make it happen. Of course, the crop he harvested, more than the corn that hid it, was marijuana. If the sheriff started poking around the place while he was gone, he may find it. Ralph Oeny would confiscate the best of it and burn the rest, just to make it look good for the state police. Henry knew Ralph would probably waste it on the whores he picked up or sell it to Buck Stanley, even though Buck thought the sheriff had it out for him. Ralph didn't, as Henry knew; he was only after Buck's stash most of the time.

Those things would have to wait though. At that time, Henry was unsure where he was or why he was there. The last thing he remembered was Jesse talking to him. Then all went dark, and he wound up there, floating in the air, suspended by nothing. There were others with him, too. Henry could hear them but was unable to make out what they were saying. They buzzed around his head like turbulent bees. Disoriented and confused, Henry attempted to reach out, at least in his mind he did. But he had no arms, or did he? Gravity and all sense of orientation had failed him, and he found himself caught in some form of vortex.

Once, when he was younger, he had seen a cow taken up in a tornado. It was the damnedest thing he had ever seen. Betsy, the milking cow he adored, was just pulled from the earth, right where she stood. His dad found her a day later, two miles away, torn into three pieces and scattered across a field. Other debris was mixed around her, including other animals with their body parts all laced together and strewn out to where you couldn't tell what was what. The only way they could tell Betsy was among them was because of the farm identification tag on her ear. Buzzing in that vortex, he knew how she felt, only he was alive. He focused on some of the voices in the swarm. Henry could finally make out what they were saying.

"Rebecca, feed us!"

He felt hungry suddenly but different than the way he remembered. He longed for sustenance, feeling as though he wanted something he couldn't touch.

"Rebecca has arrived!" he heard them say, and felt a warm presence come over him.

The sensation he couldn't explain, like what he thought it may have felt to be breast fed by his momma when he was a child. He looked to the floor below and saw a girl, young and beautiful, with olive-colored skin and eyes like ebony. She reminded him of a Native-American girl he knew when he was kid. She wore a thin robe, but as she walked up onto a stage of some kind, she removed it and sat cross-legged with no clothing on at all. Sitting the way she was, Henry thought she took on more of an appearance of an Egyptian princess or gypsy.

Whoever she was, he knew he wanted her, as did the rest of the people there. She held up her hands, waving the others toward her.

Henry followed, the urge to be with her stronger than anything he'd ever felt.

"Come to me, my children!"

Henry felt as though he were being pulled downward although he wasn't sure, as up or down in that place made no sense. He realized he was in a tent, seeing the canvas ceiling and wood columns in the middle of the room. His arms and legs felt incredibly light, as though they were disconnected from him. He looked at one of them and saw it to be true; the arm was above him, mixed in with other arms. What the hell was happening to him?

He reached for his neck to see if it was connected as well. He felt it there, just the way he remembered. His head and torso were all together; only his legs and arms were gone. Meaty stumps sprouted from his shoulders and hips where the arms and legs had once been. Although they were hovering above, he could still feel them. It was a strange and wondrous sensation, like he was having an out of body experience. He supposed he was.

The parts stopped only feet away from where Rebecca sat. Henry's torso hovered as, one by one, his appendages came to rest in their intended places. The legs fell into place first, flesh connecting to flesh. The sinewy tendons and muscles were like something Henry remembered seeing from his biology class when he was in high school. He'd never seen anything so strange before. The arms were last, and once they melded with his body, he stretched, raising his arms over his head.

Crowds of people formed around him: men, women, and children. Some he recognized, town folk he'd known all his life. Greta Oeny and Buck Stanley to name a few, all doing with their bodies the same thing his did. There were others, too. Men sporting mustaches and beards out of their time, like something from long ago. Women with hairstyles from different time periods. No one wore clothing, him included, but nobody seemed to mind. They were all fixated on the queen who took the stage.

Henry followed the rest of the crowd and made his way forward. Everyone gathered around Rebecca, laying hands on her as she relaxed, letting the energy from her children—yes, he felt as though he were her child—flow through her. It was exhilarating to watch and to experience. Rebecca moaned, as did the crowd. Henry's body exploded with pleasure. An orgasmic experience was how he'd describe it, and it was the best he'd ever had. Following Rebecca was all he ever wanted to do, to please her was paramount.

The McCarthy boys, making their way from the back of the crowd, lay their hands on Henry's shoulders. He regarded them, overjoyed with their presence.

"Boys! Isn't this great? I've never felt so good."

"It's wonderful, Daddy. Soon though, Rebecca will have a job for you. Your old pal, Sy Sutton, should be here soon. Allen didn't get him, but you can welcome him when he gets here," Jesse said.

"Sy, huh? It's been a while since we talked, but if I remember, he's a stubborn one. But with some proper persuasion, I feel he'll come around. I did."

"That's right, Daddy. He'll come around, and we'll take care of the little woman he's been hanging out with, too. Rebecca wants them both, front and center," Nathan said.

Engrossed in their revelry, Henry and his boys failed to notice a ghost near the back of the tent, one they would have recognized, carrying half a baby in her arms. Nicole watched intently as the crowd continued in the throes of pleasure, but she was especially focused on her family.

As Rebecca sat in meditation on the stage, Sage eased up to her and knelt by her side. She didn't regard him, only spoke aloud. "You come to ask forgiveness from your queen?"

"Yes. I don't know what happened back there. I was under some kind an of influence or something."

"I told you to mind the dead. They will play tricks on you. They've come for me before. This isn't the first time. They tend to gather every hundred years or so. I know how to defeat them. It's you I'm worried about."

"You needn't fret over me. You are my queen. I know this. I'm with you to the end."

"Oh, Sage, your father said the same thing before he was beguiled. Your family has a history of strength but also weakness. But I must have you on my side if I'm to survive. My blood helped rejuvenate Allen, and he's become a good general. But even so, he needs your help and guidance if he's to prosper."

"Yes, I know." His thoughts went to his daddy and the bloody head he took the hat from. He wondered if she'd had a similar conversation with him.

"Why are you thinking of him? The betrayer?"

Sage realized his thoughts were an open book to her, so he closed off any of Sadie. "I don't know. He's come to mind lately is all."

"Yes, I see. There's something else there, too. Something you may be hiding from me?"

"No, my queen, nothing at all. I'll go find Allen, discuss your plan with him," he said, nervously.

"Good. Mind me, Sage. Your father betrayed me and regretted it. Don't do the same."

"Never, my queen."

Once he felt he was far enough away, he thought of Sadie, of his family. Had his daddy been trying to escape Rebecca? Why did he have little memory of him? Apparently, Rebecca had nothing but disdain for the man. But who was right? He needed to find Allen. Maybe he was the connection to it all of this.

Allen entered the tent to the sound of a raucous cacophony, not only from the parts but the crowd gathering on the floor. People from town were flooding in from all directions, pulling back flaps of fabric and placing stakes in the ground to create side entrances. The blue flame in the center was the only light in the structure, and it gave off enough luminescence to allow the people to see while keeping the parts hidden in the darkness above.

Samson was gathered near the front along with Buck Stanley and Harley, as well as some bearded men with tattoos, to act as crowd control for Rebecca. The people milled about aimlessly, not really understanding where they were or why, but an occasional straggler would make it to the steps and start to ascend toward her. When they did, they were immediately redirected by Samson and his crew.

Allen noticed the sheriff was there, too.

The man talked to Samson before leaving through the back of the tent as if directed to do something. Rebecca really did have control of the town, if she had the authorities as well.

Allen smiled when he saw Sage motioning for him by the corner of the stage. Rhonda left him, hovering above the crowd, making her way to Rebecca.

The crowd was thick, and Allen could have just as easily flew above them as Rhonda did, but he chose instead to push his way through. He was a few feet from Sage when the man turned for the shadows behind the stage. Puzzled, Allen followed him. When Allen turned the corner, he saw Sage leaving through the back of the tent. Before he exited completely, he turned and gestured for Allen to follow him outside. Allen didn't understand why but, seeing it was Sage, had no reason to doubt the man's intentions.

As he stepped outside, he saw the sheriff talking to some people in the yard by the Owens' house. It looked to be his deputies, but it was hard to tell. Night had enveloped the area, and no moon peeked from the clouds. The wind had grown stronger as well, and Allen noticed the edges of the tent fluttering in response. He made out the silhouette of Sage near the edge of the woods. Sage continued to walk, not letting Allen catch up to him but keeping within sight.

Allen was starting to become frustrated by the time he noticed Sage finally stopping near a clearing. The area was out of sight of the tent. Only the top pole in the middle of the structure could be seen. As Allen's eyes adjusted to the dark, he could see they were in more of a valley than a clearing. One large tree with branches snaking out in different directions, all low to the ground, stood in stark contrast to the rest around it. Twelve stones wrapped in a circle around its base, glowing lightly, enough to allow Allen to see.

Sage stood in front of the tree, welcoming a group of ghosts. They blinked—the best way he could describe it—in and out of existence, just like he'd seen in the parking lot of Sam's. As he focused on the sight, he saw Sage was talking to his mom.

Sage raised his arms and spoke some words Allen didn't understand. The tree pulsed with light and the stones glowed brighter around it. The Sadie ghost blinked in and out, as did the rest of the ghosts gathered, then she disappeared and reappeared a few feet from Allen. She smiled, motioning him toward her.

Allen regarded Sage indignantly. "What are you doing? Aren't these the same entities conspiring against Rebecca? Are you betraying her?"

"No, Allen, you have to realize, I've changed my way of thinking, thanks to my granddaughter here."

"Granddaughter? She's my mom, at least I think she is. I'm not sure if any of this is real."

"She is, Allen, and all this is real. Search your heart, the part Rebecca doesn't have yet. You'll find it there, tucked away, a small section of what's left of your family. You and I come from a long line of people who are sent to make things right. There's a cosmic battle going on here, and Sadie has helped me to see the role I play in it. That goes for you as well. You're my grandson, and I need you to set things right in this town and all the others Rebecca intends to take down."

"I don't get it. Rebecca is all to me. She's in my thoughts, encompasses everything in me."

"She wants you to believe in her, Allen, so she can defeat us. You have to be stronger than her, take back what she's taken from you. "

"I believed in her, have for many years. I ignored all the things that made me who I am, even conspired against my daddy for her. Once she gets inside, she takes your heart from you and corrupts your very soul. Through my family, I've seen what she really is, and now I want it to end. It must end now, with you Allen," Sage said.

"I don't know. I feel her pulsing in me. How can I resist her?"

"Let us help you, just as we've helped your grandfather." Sadie motioned to the other ghosts around her. "These are your kin, Allen. They will show you the way."

Allen watched as each ghost circled him, all people with a familiar aura and an inviting warmth he couldn't explain. They entered his body, one by one, each with a story to tell. It was of an ancient battle, one where Rebecca was defeated but not completely. She came back, time and again, until the ghosts found her. One showed every time, although Allen didn't know her name. Rebecca mouthed it each and every time. Calypso.

Then, as the memories of battle faded, he was privileged to one last story. It was Nicole's. In it, she looked as lovely as the day he met her, smiling with her child, his child, in her arms. But there was another there, a child he didn't know about.

"Allen, Rhonda killed me to get to our children. She thought she finished the job, but she was unaware we had twins, one of our children lived. She destroyed the womb, but the child lives on. No one knows about her, not even my family. She's a Jane doe in the city of Lexington. You or your family must find her before Rebecca does."

When the ghosts left him, they gathered near the tree, each one attached to one of the stones. As they disappeared into the rocks, they left only Sage standing before him.

Allen looked at him. "Now what do we do? Samson and his people won't let us get anywhere near Rebecca, and all the people in there, how do we save them?"

"We won't save them. At least not all of them. There's no way we can do it and defeat her as well. There's no doubt some souls will perish tonight. But we can save as many as possible."

"At least let me get to my family. My sister and nephew. My dad if he comes back. They can be spared anyway."

"Okay, while I distract her, get them out of harm's way. When the time is right, the spirits will gather, then we will go below into the mine. It's where she'll retreat to."

"The ghosts, huh? Even the one I saw in my mind? Calypso, I think it was?"

"Especially that one. I defeated her once before with Samson's help for Rebecca, but not this time. I've invoked her name, and Calypso can have her, along with the rest of them. My daddy protected my family a hundred years ago by sparing my child, even though it cost him his life. I'm going to repay the debt. Did you see anything relating to children in your vision?"

"Only that I have a child I didn't know about. No one knows about her, but once this is over, I'm going to find her."

"Well, I suppose the child has lived on again. Rebecca obviously doesn't know. I guess we both have something to fight for now, Grandson. We both have our parts to play."

"Yeah, I guess we do, Grandpa," Allen replied smiling.

Allen left the clearing with Sage and walked toward the tent. He turned back once to see the small stones vanishing into the ground along with the tree, leaving only dense forest where they stood.

Chapter Sixteen

Come One, Come All

Cars were lined bumper to bumper on the small road leading to the Owens' farm. Sheriff Oeny had his car parked at the entrance to the farm, blue lights flashing in the near darkness. His plan to go out there and talk to the occupants of the tent was derailed by the sudden onslaught of vehicles descending on the place. Instead of the sheriff, he'd become a traffic scout. The side roads were also buzzing with activity. ATVs, their motors screaming, cruised along the trails in the woods nearby. Ralph saw them, but paid no attention, his priority on the traffic. He had limited options. With the demise of Bill Pence, he only had two deputies to spare, Sam and Rolo. He didn't count Carla, because she was needed on dispatch.

Reports were coming in of traffic bottlenecking main street from the IGA to the Owens' farm, all because of that Sage fella. *What the hell was going on?* It was the biggest jam he'd seen since the circus came to town the year before. Ralph thought it might even be bigger. He tried to hail one of the cars, attempting to veer it into the field and park, but the driver completely ignored him and drove the car into the Owens' front yard, nearly missing Bob in the process. The occupants of the vehicle got out and blindly walked to the tent.

Several other cars proceeded to do the same, parking haphazardly wherever the mood seemed to indicate. It was turning into a big mess, and Ralph was sure he'd be responsible for cleaning it all up. Trying to direct the next cars and failing miserably, he stopped when he heard dispatch trying to reach him.

"101? Ralph, you there? Over?"

He reached in the car and retrieved the radio mic.

"This is Ralph, Carla, over?"

"Ralph, there's a disturbance in the woods near the Owens farm."

"I'm here now. What's the problem?"

"There's a report of an off-road vehicle crashing into the side of a car out there. Nobody's hurt, but Gary Rutherford is pretty pissed."

"Carla, I'm pretty busy here. Can one of the boys take care of it, over?" Ralph heard the impatience in his voice building.

"Sorry, Ralph. They're all busy here in town. This traffic snarl is taking its toll on everyone."

"Okay, okay. I'll get it. Over and out."

"Thanks, Ralph," Carla said, trailing off.

Ralph looked in the direction of the woods and could see people moving near the end of the trail head. No sounds were coming from the ATVs. Ralph figured he didn't need to stay there anyway, considering how the traffic directing was going. He grabbed his walkie, pulled his belt and pants up over his considerable paunch, and started walking.

At the scene of the accident, Ralph saw the car, the front end pulled into the trail. From the looks of things, it was attempting to turn around. The ATV was firmly attached to the steaming grill. Ralph heard commotion on the other side of the vehicle and got there in time to see Gary Rutherford holding a boy in a headlock. Another kid was hitting his back, doing nothing to faze the man, as Gary was North of 350 pounds solid. The only effect the boy was having was further angering Gary.

The boys Ralph recognized as Sam and Toby Schneider from over on Lockton Road, off Hackworth Hollow. Their daddy had a farm there. Ralph had taken them home more than a couple of times for ripping up the town with their ATV.

"That's enough!" Ralph shouted.

Sam, the one hitting Gary on the back, stopped immediately. But Gary wasn't about to let the red-faced Toby go.

"Gary! Stop. You're going to kill him," Ralph said, impatiently.

Gary noticed Ralph and let Toby go. The kid landed on his knees, grabbing his throat and gasping for breath.

"Ralph, these little sons of bitches had it coming. They's been causing trouble in town for a while now!"

"That may be so, but they're also underage. If you hurt one of 'em, you'll go to jail. Now settle down, and we'll see what's going on."

Gary hung his head in defeat and gave Ralph his side of the story, beginning with him pulling off the road to turn around.

"I got you, and I'll write everything down, but the vehicles will have to stay where they are for now. There's no way a rollback could get out here with all the cars on the road." Ralph pointed to the snarl.

"You mean our side by side's going to be stuck here for the rest of the night?" Toby retorted.

"If'n you was watching where you's going, it wouldn't be, you little asswipe," Gary sneered.

"Just settle down. We'll get one out here as soon as we can."

"Well, I guess I could walk on down to the revival. It's not too far from here. It's where I was headed anyway," Gary said.

"C'mon, Toby, I guess we got to go back and tell Daddy what happened. He'll be pissed." Sam lowered his head.

Ralph smiled, regarding the pair of young men. *At least the boys are taking some responsibility. There may be hope for them yet.*

He turned back to address Gary, maybe talk some sense into him about going to the revival, but Ralph noticed the man was gone. He scanned the wooded area and saw Gary stepping onto the Owen's front yard, headed in the direction of the revival along with several others aimlessly stumbling towards the tent. *Too late for talking now.*

He checked over the crash vehicles, jotted down some information, and started back for his cruiser. Halfway through the woods back to the Owens' farm, he saw a large man at the edge of Bob's front lawn. He had something in his hand. It looked to be an inhaler, the kind they use for asthmatics.

He was sucking on it, nursing it as though it were his mother's tit. The man moved his head slowly side to side as if he were scanning the woods, then looked at Ralph and smiled, making a sawing motion across his neck. The sheriff froze, uneasy with the message the man was sending, and stepped out of sight behind a tree. He unsnapped his weapon from the holster, stepping into the open, the gun drawn in front of him. Ralph pointed it in the direction of the man, but he was gone.

He contemplated what had just happened then changed focus to the amount of cars in the Owens' front yard and the mess it'd become. He needed to do something about it if he were to investigate the tent situation. He keyed up the small mic from his walkie and spoke.

"Carla? I know Sam and Rolo are busy, but they need to stop what they're doing and get out here. This situation is getting out of control fast! Over?"

"Will do, Ralph. Be careful, over?"

"Over and out." He shook his head in frustration.

Ralph took a step forward, trying to quietly navigate the forest toward the Owens' farm, a useless endeavor as every twig or leaf he encountered snapped and crunched below him. To make matters worse, small saplings were catching the bottom of his pants and impeding his progress. Ralph evaded most of the little trees and continued until the fabric on his trousers caught and wouldn't let go. He held onto a tree and pulled at his pants leg, but it didn't budge. He pulled harder, trying to free his pants from the snag but oddly encountered resistance. His leg was being pulled down.

"The hell?"

Something at the bottom of his pants, defied explanation. A hand was groping for purchase, working its way up his leg, but to Ralph's horror, there was no body attached to it. The appendage was large and meaty, belonging to someone big at one time. He shook his leg furiously, trying to free the offending thing, but it held on, digging into his leg as it ascended toward his crotch. He lowered his gun toward it but thought better of the idea.

Once it reached his midsection, Ralph grabbed it and tried to free it from his clothing. The hand clamped tighter, then twisted. Ralph howled in pain, pushing at the hand, then smacking it with the butt of the pistol, attempting to stop the onslaught. The hand held on with incredible strength.

He threw his head back as white dots blurred his vision. Waves of nausea gripped him, and he turned his head, emptying the contents of his stomach, feeling like he would pass out. The hand let go, and Ralph fell to his knees by the tree, gasping for wind.

Someone laughed as Ralph tried to regain his composure, a big deep belly laugh, just above him. Weakly, he raised his head to see the big man from earlier, only some parts were missing. His head was floating, suspended by nothing, in the air above Ralph. The man's arms un-

believably whirled around him in a sort of vortex. They stopped and
with lightning speed hurtled toward Ralph like heat seeking missiles at
their intended target. He screamed, releasing what little air remained
in his lungs, as the arms ripped through his chest.

Patty and Sy drove toward his place, the opposite direction of the
street party. Sy stopped the car.

"What is it?" she asked.

"You know we can't run away. We have to go back."

"Sy, we were nearly killed back there. Maybe we should call the
police first before we go back."

"What good would it do. All the local law enforcement were there
for the show. You know they'll be at the tent, too. As far as killing me,
Allen wouldn't do such a thing. He doesn't have it in him. There's no
way."

"Sy, you have to realize he's not who he was. I don't know what
Rhonda has done to him, but he's not the same. I barely knew him
before he came to me as a comatose patient, and I can see that. She's
done something to him."

*She is making sense, and she didn't see what I did, my son's hand
coming loose from his body. How is something like that even possible?*
"You may be right, Patty, but that's even more of a reason for me to
go back for him. I need to talk some sense into him before I lose him
again. I didn't break him out of the hospital for nothing. I don't think
it's too late. I think he'll come around as long as I can have a stab at
talking to him."

"Well, you know I'm in either way. You go and I follow."

He smiled at her and gave her hand a gentle squeeze, then lightly kissed her on the lips. Patty responded by kissing him firmly and deeply before releasing.

"All right then. Let's go save my son...again."

Sy pulled into the parking lot of Sam's grocery, staring at the line of barely moving traffic on the road to the Owens' farm. The two deputies who were attempting to direct people to other routes obviously had no idea what they were doing. They seem flustered, screaming and yelling at people who were paying them no attention at all. Sy knew them—Rolo and Sam, two of Salt Licks finest. *Those two couldn't wipe their asses without Ralph's help.* Sy watched as Sam reached into his car and answered the radio, then the two deputies got into the patrol car and sped away along the shoulder, lights blaring.

Sy saw a break and decided to follow them, driving closely behind the patrol car, Sy and Patty were within a mile of the Owens' farm when a car veered from the line, narrowly missing the deputies but stopping Sy from going any farther. The people in the car stepped out and began walking toward the tent revival, their eyes focused forward as if in some hypnotic trance. Sy shut the car off and looked at his passenger.

"You got your hiking shoes on, Patty? Looks like we're walking from here."

"I'm a nurse; I always wear comfortable shoes."

Sy scanned the area for the best way to get to the tent but saw nothing. The cars were wedged in so tightly that there were no openings they could go through. He decided the best way would be to walk along the shoulder until they got to the entrance of the Owens' farm then go through their front yard. Patty followed, and within a few minutes they were on the small, graveled road by the farm. The sun had fallen behind the hill, plunging the field into darkness save for the lights of the parked vehicles. Most were still running, left alone, the occupants so entranced in the event they didn't care.

The tent was buzzing with excitement as people entered from both sides. Faint light filtered out from the slits where the canvas met. There didn't seem to be any electric going to it. It was the real deal, an old-fashioned tent revival with lights from lamps or fires. From inside the tent, screams penetrated the night like some vengeful banshee looking for souls. Sy supposed it was exactly what was happening. Weren't revivals for bringing in new souls to the fold? By the looks of it, the whole town was in for a raising.

The patrol car the deputies were driving was parked on the front lawn of the Owens' house, empty of its occupants, the blue lights still on. But no one paid them any attention, no more than on the road. Sam and Rolo were nowhere to be seen, and an uneasiness gripped Sy as he went forward.

"What do you think, Patty?"

"I think this is the creepiest thing I've ever seen. I don't like it. Can't we just leave?"

Sy walked toward the crowd of people clamoring to get inside. "Too late now, but I have a plan. We could follow them in, get lost in the crowd. Then nobody could spot us?"

"I guess but be careful. Allen and Rhonda didn't have too much trouble before finding us at the street party, remember?"

"How could I forget? I'll be careful. C'mon."

Sy blended in with the crowd of people entering the tent. He saw Sally and Tom walking ahead of them with Eli right behind. He tried to get closer but was afraid he'd lose Patty in the process. The people seemed to be hovering toward the middle of the structure around a glow of light. There was movement near the top and a strange buzzing sound like a hive of bees. Sy was finding it difficult to keep up with Patty as the massive crowd pushed forward. He stepped back and put his arm around her, pushing her to the side and out of the melee of people toward the back of the tent.

"We'll never find him in this crowd. Let's go outside. Maybe we can make a short cut."

Thick leather straps held the sections of tent together along the areas where large ropes were tied to stakes in the ground, keeping the thing from flying away. Sy untied a couple straps from the bottom, and the wind immediately slapped the free piece of canvas against the outside wall. He grabbed for Patty and guided her through the opening before ducking through himself, hoping no one heard the commotion. It was doubtful as the din inside was near deafening.

Sy and Patty stepped into the outside darkness. The woods nearby gave the background an extra blanket of blackness. The sky was cloudy, covering the moon completely. The wind died down and insects began chirping loudly in the humid air. Sy swatted his ear at the high-pitched whine of a mosquito trying to land, then listened as other noises made themselves present nearby, most notably the sound of men struggling.

Patty and Sy eased around the corner to see Ralph Oeny holding both of his deputies off their feet. The young men were wide-eyed and scared as they struggled to get free. Ralph threw one of them on the ground. It looked like Sam, but it was hard to tell in the dark. He then concentrated his full attention on the other. The man screamed, then made a gurgling sound from deep within his throat as Ralph thrust his hand through the deputy's chest. Ralph, his jaws out of place like they were broken, pulled his hand out and bit into the pulpy meat of the deputy's heart.

The other deputy opened fire, emptying six rounds into the back of Sheriff Oeny as fast as he could pull the trigger. Oeny flinched and dropped his victim before turning on the deputy who shot him. An arm flew from his body, striking the deputy in the chest. Sy watched, too shocked to turn away but trying to get a grasp on the brutality he saw. He reached for Patty, pulling her close to shield her, maybe to hide himself as well. No, he was sure he was hiding his eyes. He felt as though he would vomit.

Patty pulled away from him instead and watched the bloody scene unfold in front of her, appearing to be undeterred by the violence.

"Don't try and protect me, Sy. I'm a nurse, and I've seen my fair share of blood. I can tell you one thing, though." She shivered. "I've never seen anything remotely as gruesome as that."

"We need to find another way," Sy said.

They turned around but didn't get far, met by an opposing figure. Patty, startled by the intruder, let out a small scream, but Sy felt somewhat relieved. He knew the guy.

"Henry? What are you doing here?"

"I'm enjoying life, Sy, and you will too, very soon." Henry smiled, the look on his face unnerving.

Henry McCarthy rarely ever smiled, but he looked beaming at that moment. Something wasn't right.

"I think you two should come with me. I have some people I want you to meet."

"If it's just the same, Henry, me and Patty have somewhere to be. Right, Patty?"

Patty didn't speak, only nodded and gripped Sy's hand.

"Okay then, see you later, Henry."

Henry stepped toward Sy and grabbed him by the lapel of his shirt. "I could rip your heart out and eat it, right where you stand, but someone else wants the pleasure of that task."

From behind Patty, two other figures appeared from the darkness. It was Henry's sons. Sy should have known they wouldn't be far away. Jesse grabbed Patty by the arm.

"Hey, Sutton, your boy's been looking for you, and I'm sure you've been looking for him. Now's your chance to find him. What do you say?"

Patty struggled against his iron grip. "Do we have a choice?"

Nathan stepped beside her. "What do you think?"

"Then it's settled. We're all going to see Allen and the Sage. After Allen told him about you, he's been dying to meet you," Henry said.

Each McCarthy boy grabbed Sy and Patty's arms and led them inside the tent with Henry following. Behind the stage, Allen and Rhonda waited.

"Hey, dad, good of you to come back. I wondered why you ran away so fast."

Sy wrestled from the arm of his captor and straightened his shirt. He looked his son in the eye. "I think we know why I got away the first time. Your mom had something to do with it."

"Mom? Dad, Mom died a while ago. Don't try anything stupid. It won't do any good. Besides, you'll love what Rebecca gives. You and your girlfriend." Allen raised his arm, making a fist. "Now, dad, where were we?"

"Allen? You haven't introduced me."

Allen stopped in mid-swing and turned to Sage and Samson standing behind him. "Sure, Sage, this is my dad, Sy Sutton, the one I told you about, and his girlfriend, Patty, I think it is?"

"Yes, I'm Patty. I took care of you in the hospital. You don't remember, do you?"

"Miss, I remember very little from that time, least of all you. Now, Sage, if you don't mind, I'd like to bring them into the fold."

Sage smiled. "It's okay, Allen. We need not be in a rush. I feel they need a little more coaxing anyway. Let them see the service and see what transpires. All good things come to those who wait for Rebecca."

Allen hesitated. He smiled at Sy, releasing him from his grasp.

"Good. Now come, Sy Sutton. See the spectacle of Rebecca." Sage waved his hand in the direction of the stage.

Sy and Patty, realizing they had little choice, stepped forward toward the stage. The McCarthy boys, Henry, and Allen followed, then Sage and Samson. On the stage, Sy could hear the roar of the crowd and the buzzing he'd heard before. The strangest sound coming from above. He saw no bees, but the noise was definitely the same. Then, Sage stopped them from going any farther, making the pair stand to the side while he took center stage.

The scene was chaotic. People were falling over each other as Sage began to preach. His body glowed as he rose into the air until he was hovering above the crowd. They fell to their knees, grasping their hands in a makeshift prayer position. Sy hadn't been to church since Sadie died, but he was sure there was no preacher he knew or had ever seen who could do something like that. But then again, demons could play tricks on people, luring them to their doom. It seemed reminiscent of such a thing.

"Let us make glorious noise, my people!" Sage shouted over the crowd, then singing "Let the Circle be Unbroken."

The people sung with him, shouting praises to him. Sy and Patty watched the whole thing uncomfortably from their corner of the stage. They were flanked to either side by the McCarthys and Allen. Samson was behind them. The only one missing was Rhonda. She had been with Allen earlier, but they hadn't seen her since they entered the tent. Sy felt uneasy knowing she was on the loose somewhere and worried for Patty's safety. But there was nowhere to go. The only thing to do was ride it out and wait for their break, if they got one.

"Let loose your shackles and be who you are." Sage told the crowd.

The light from his body glowed brighter as it illuminated the upper tent, making the ceiling visible. Sy had no explanation for what he was seeing. Heads, arms, and legs, all sorts of human body parts flying in formation, created the buzzing sound he'd heard earlier. Then, the crowd began to unclothe, complying to Sage's command.

It was a scene Sy could have done without. He knew many of those people, all good citizens, most very modest. The spell Sage had on them had to be powerful. He saw Greta Oeny stripping her clothes off, an image he would have trouble purging from his head. Sally was on the fringe of the crowd, and Sy saw her clothes start to fall off as well, but before she was completely disrobed, the crowd swallowed her up. Thankfully, he couldn't see her, as some things would scar a dad. Why wasn't the whole thing affecting him and Patty? No answer was coming. The whole thing was fucked up.

"To God be the glory! Do you feel the power here tonight? In this house, sin is no more! For the wages of sin is death, and I can assure you, brothers and sisters, death will be defeated!" Sage bellowed to the crowd.

In response to him, the mixed parts swooped into the crowd, the heads gnawing and biting, the arms grabbing and pulling people to the ground. Several of the parts began to meld together until they became whole people. Muscle and tendons formed when one part would meet another. Blood fell across the skin near where the parts connected, absorbing like a sponge into the skin. Once whole, they jammed their hands through the chest of a random person, pulling the heart out and eating it with disjointed jaws. Blood spewed onto the ground. The whole spectacle like some war movie.

Instead of screaming in agony, though, as Sy would expect them to, the crowd seemed to be welcoming the onslaught. He turned his head away, unable to control his nausea anymore. Sy heaved onto the floor of the stage. He heard Henry laughing at his lack of fortitude.

"My children, you have been chosen for the army to lead us into the promised land! Rebecca will be here soon, and she will give us what we want!"

The ground quaked, sending people falling into the chairs and knocking them over. Sy placed his hands on his knees to steady himself and looked into the crowd again. He saw Sally laying on the ground with Eli close beside her. Their bodies were intact, and he was grateful they weren't among the victims of the bloodbath.

He glanced at Patty and saw she was just as frightened of what was happening. Her eyes were wide, taking in the whole spectacle. They had to get out of there and get some help. The town was dying right in front of him, and he could do nothing about it. Coming back there was a definite mistake. It seemed too late for Allen and maybe the rest of his family, too, as Sy watched in dismay. There were too many around him, and even if he could get free, what about Patty? No, he'd have to wait a little longer. Then, he heard a commotion toward the entrance of the tent, a man screaming something.

"Stop this abomination! You, sir, are an apostate! A charlatan!"

Sy stood on his tiptoes and craned his neck to see who it was. Pastor Mooney from the Methodist church stood there, Bible in hand, looking to do some spiritual warfare. Sage, flying above the man, frowned. Mooney stood his ground, seeming to be unmoved by Sage's display of ability.

"You, who are the hypocrite of all ages, come to tell me how to bring people to the light?" Sage pointed at the pastor.

Mooney looked over the crowd and cringed at all the blood he saw. Bodies were strewn before him, their chest cavities caved in and entrails falling onto the ground. Perhaps he'd misjudged his effectiveness. The Sage raised his hands and laughed as the ground quaked. Then, the bloodied bodies began to move, their parts separating and crawling along the ground, clawing their way to the ankles of the pastor. Mooney jumped and danced, trying to break free of them, but they continued to climb. He screamed. the ground shook again, and the parts stopped. Everything stopped.

The dirt floor beneath the pastor began to fissure and a large crack opened below him. A tentacle, long like a Leviathan of the sea, protruded out of the ground, shooting into the top of the tent. Pastor Mooney gasped. Sage laughed, joyfully pronouncing the thing from the earth.

"Behold! Rebecca rises."

Chapter Seventeen

Revival

The large tentacle writhed, the tip swirling in circular motions at the top of the tent. Several of the parts, old and new converts, fell around Rebecca, attaching to the octopus like arms, melding into it. Their faces could be seen underneath the skin as though a veil were over them. They laughed crazily in unison. Mooney fell to his knees, his eyes wide with terror, the Bible in front of him.

Greta Oeny had been watching the pastor with interest. She had been with him in his chambers on more than one occasion, after all. Before she joined the rest, she figured a little fun was in order.

She stepped over to Mooney, her naked body jiggling with delight as she grabbed him by the hair and pulled his head to face her. Her jaws dropped open and her mouth got wider as rows of teeth formed. The look on his face was surprise and sheer terror as he screamed. Greta didn't bite into him, though. She liked to play with her prey first. Greta mashed his face against her body and rubbed her ample breasts all over the pastor. He attempted to pull away, but her grip was too strong.

"Remember those, Mooney? You sure spent a lot of time there. Maybe you could spend more?"

She held him tightly and raised him to standing until he looked her in the eye. Her mouth grew larger as the teeth, too numerous to count, faced the pastor. He winced at what he knew would come.

"Please, no. I don't deserve this," he said.

"No, what you don't deserve is to be with Rebecca, but I'll give you to her anyway."

Greta laughed as she took a bite from his shoulder and threw Pastor Mooney toward Rebecca. He screamed in pain as he fell to his knees in front of the tentacle. Blood poured from his wound, and Mooney saw the tentacle rise from the ground, separating and hovering into the air, leaving a female standing where it had been.

The ground sealed up under her, and Rebecca stood there, naked, hair flowing over her body. She grinned as her mouth opened larger than humanly possible. From her back, smaller tentacles formed, reaching forward, and taking Mooney by the neck. They wrapped around him, tightening as he gasped. He reached for his neck, clawing at the offending ropes, but he couldn't budge them. His cheeks bulged and reddened until he could no longer breathe. Blood seeped from his eyes as Rebecca's alien appendages tightened further until his head was separated from his body. Pastor Mooney's detached head rolled across the floor as his body slumped in a pile, stopping in front of a laughing Greta. Her belly jiggled with each gyration.

She picked up the head and laughed at the wide-eyed, crazed expression frozen on the deceased pastor's face. "Oh well, maybe you weren't good enough for Rebecca after all."

She then threw the head into the air as the McCarthy boys, along with Henry, levitated from the stage to grab it, tossing it into the parts above. The sound of angry bees droned throughout the tent as they devoured the bloody treat presented to them. Henry floated to Greta as she rose in the air to meet him. Their naked bodies embraced, rolling in an erotic melee that would make the least squeamish person gag with revulsion. Jesse and Nathan remained nearby, laughing uncontrollably at the show in front of them.

"Get after it, Daddy," Jesse called out.

Sy watched the sickening spectacle in front of him, knowing he'd never get those images out of his head. He realized they had to make their escape soon, or they'd be next. His captors were distracted, cheering, and caught up in the blood lust in front of them, Sy figured it might be the best time to try. He nudged Patty and motioned for the back of the stage with his head. They eased backward toward the steps, turning slowly, but Samson was upon them before they even got close.

"Going somewhere?" the large man said.

Another figure stepped from the dark behind the stage to back Samson up. Sy watched as his old friend Buck Stanley stood there, eyes glowing and mouth opening wide. It wasn't the Buck he knew, of course, and just as it was with Henry, he had no reason to think he'd be merciful.

"I don't want any trouble with you. We'll be leaving now. We can come back for Allen later."

"You won't need to. I'm going to let you stay around."

Rhonda was beside him, prodding Sally and Eli onto the stage. Thankfully, they'd managed to partially clothe themselves with their underwear, but seeing the pitiful shape of their dirty bodies as they shivered uncontrollably produced a sickening feeling in the pit of Sy's stomach.

"Allen, c'mon, son. That's your sister and nephew. You can't hurt them. Take me, but leave them." Sy stepped forward.

Patty grasped his hand and stood beside him. "Me too."

"Don't worry, there are many layers to Rebecca's house. All of you can stay." Sage stepped in beside Allen and Rhonda.

"Dad, I'm sorry. I don't know what happened. We were at the street party then here. I don't know where Tom is." Sally cried and clutched Eli closer to her.

"Fear not. A little longer, and it will all be a dream, one you cannot wake up from. I'll take it from here, Allen," Sage said.

"No, Sage. They're my family, and I should take care of them. Let me make them one with Rebecca."

"I'm afraid I must insist," Sage replied.

As they decided who would dispatch Sy and company, Rebecca cheered triumphantly, watching the parts swarming the crowd. She stopped, though, when she noticed a figure working her way through the people, coming directly for her.

The woman smiled as she passed through Greta Oeny. Greta began sizzling, her skin popping like bacon frying. She screamed in agony, a blood curdling affair as she burst into flame. No one around her noticed except Rebecca who had her eyes trained on the woman, realizing who she was. An ancient figure from long before, one she thought she'd never see again.

"Calypso? But how could you be here? Unless...Sage!" Rebecca's voice thundered over all of them. "I told you not to be compromised."

Sage turned to Rebecca and saw her surrounded by ghosts. Sepia colored apparitions flowed around her body, laying hands on her skin, burning it with each touch. One ghost who stood out to Sage was directing the others. He smiled as he watched Calypso do her dirty work.

The blue flame in the middle of the tent began to show signs of red and orange. It rose then fell, going out completely, plunging the tent into total darkness. The parts above screamed in agony, running blind into each other as the large tentacle, holding suspended above, crashed to the ground, releasing the parts. They rolled and clawed along the dirt, confused by the assault, as a large fissure appeared in the ground and began extending in spider webbed cracks along the inside of the tent.

Samson, seeing the ghost as well, gave a look of disgust to Sage. "What have you done?"

Samson ran to Rebecca. He wrapped his body around her to shield her from the onslaught. The ghostly bodies immediately attacked, and his skin sizzled and popped as well. Momentarily caught off guard, Allen, Buck, and Rhonda watched dumbfounded at the turn of events. But then Rhonda focused on Sage, her brow furrowed.

"Allen! Quickly, we have to get them to safety." Sage said.

"Allen? You too?" Rhonda's voice dripped with disdain at this betrayal. She lunged forward, grabbing Patty. "I should have torn you apart earlier, you fucking bitch. Now, I'll eat you while your boyfriend watches."

Allen jumped forward and reached for Rhonda, but instead of being captured, she pulled away, holding tighter to Patty. Sy watched, helpless to do anything.

"Rhonda, it's me you want, not her," Allen said. "I know what you did to Nicole. Let's you and I end this now."

"Fuck you, Allen! You don't know anything. I made you what you are. If not for me, you'd never have met Rebecca."

He looked at her with troubled eyes. "I know you did, but now I need to undo it. This thing I've become is all wrong."

"No, that's crazy talk. I don't care about you. If you want to go a different direction, then I don't care. It doesn't change the fact Nurse Pain-in-the-ass here dies!"

Sage grabbed Sy by the wrist, pleading for him to follow as he led Sally and Eli from harm's way. Instead of following, Sy pulled away, making a leap for Patty, but before he could reach her, Allen intervened, grabbing Rhonda by the throat. Caught off balance, Rhonda reeled backward, releasing her grasp of Patty as she and Allen went rolling onto the ground off the stage. Patty lay shaken but unharmed., Sy held her for a moment, allowing her shaking body to meld into his for comfort, before helping her to her feet.

The McCarthy boys watched the fight before them. They realized their queen was in trouble, her tentacled arms waving wildly throughout the tent as strange black and white blurs were seemed to be assaulting her. Strangely, Samson held her in a semi embrace, swatting crazily at the invaders. They knew Allen Sutton, the ever-present thorn in their side, had something to do with it. They'd tolerated the friend's situation with him long enough. It was time for some payback.

The pair dropped quickly onto the ground and proceeded to go to where Allen and Rhonda were fighting. Before they could reach them, a figure appeared in front of them, like some flickering film of yesteryear.

"Nicole?" Nathan said.

"The fuck?" Jesse added.

She brought a single finger to her mouth and hushed them as a half-torn baby crawled to perch on her head. The boys screamed as her hands burned them, keeping both from going any further. The baby leaped from her and wriggled down Jesse's throat, his body immediately convulsing from the onslaught.

Nathan watched in horror while trying to free himself from Nicole's grasp. Nicole released him and smiled as Jesse's body burst into flames. Nathan turned from her and stumbled, got back to his feet and tried to run, but Nicole's baby, jutting from Jesse's body, shot like a rocket toward him, catching in the small of his back. He fell to his knees, screaming.

Sy and Patty, both on wobbly legs, joined Sage and Sy's family at the bottom of the steps.

"You have to leave, now!" Sage said to them as the ground bucked and heaved below them.

"But, Allen, he needs my help," protested Sy.

"You can do nothing for him, I'll stay behind and make sure he's all right."

They headed for the edge of the tent while Sage returned to the fight. Patty grasped the canvas and pulled the side up, motioning for Sally and Eli to go under. She continued to hold it for Sy, but as the ground shook below them, he lost his balance and fell on his bottom. Sy tried to get up, grasping for any purchase he could find. He clawed his way to Patty but was stopped and instead began to be pulled backward. Patty screamed when she saw the tentacled arm wrapped around him.

"Go, Patty, take Sally and Eli. Get to safety!" he cried.

"No! Sy get my hand."

He reached for her but realized she was too far away. He felt himself being pulled backward, the ground crumbling within the tent. He watched Patty helplessly until she was obscured by darkness.

The tentacle dug into his chest, making it hard to breathe. Everything was dark, and he had no bearing of where he was, up or down. He did hear the cracking beneath him. The ground shook, and he was keenly aware he was falling, maybe not as fast as if he were jumping from a cliff, but he knew it was happening.

"Allen! I don't know where you are, but if you still love your old man, please help me."

He screamed but heard nothing. The tentacle seemed to grasp tighter, maybe to break his fall or maybe to break him, Sy wasn't sure. He did know if he didn't get free soon, the thing would tear him in two. He grabbed whatever he could, finally feeling hard ground and holding on the best he could.

He managed to hold on long enough to see his family saved, but he'd meet his end there. He knew it. It wasn't so bad. He'd managed to love two wonderful women in his lifetime, although the last had been too brief. But overall, he couldn't complain.

He took a shallow, haggard breath and prepared to die. But then, the darkness parted.

The most beautiful sight he'd ever seen appeared, and several black and white figures surrounded him. It was a comforting sight, like some old black and white movie, one he'd seen as a kid, the kind they played every year around Christmas. Remotely, he thought he may have heard a bell ring, a wonderful sound, as he felt himself slipping from consciousness.

But before he was completely out, one of the movie characters floated beside him, one he recognized immediately. It was Sadie. She looked forlornly in his eyes and reached for him, touching the appendage attempting to pull him into the pit. As she did, Sy heard a horrible scream below, then the tentacle released and fell away.

He took a much needed deep breath and renewed his grasp on the rock. But he felt his grip slipping. Small rocks fell from above, and he heard a large swooshing sound coming with them. From the area dimly lit by the still-present apparitions, he saw the tent barreling toward him. He pushed his body as close to the wall as possible. The large canvas structure fell beside him, producing a wind tunnel effect as it went by, nearly pulling him from his perch.

Sy winced as a large wooden pole hit right beside him, then tumbled below in a tangle of rope. But it wasn't done yet. A piece of the rope had unwound and spun furiously, acting as a whip, lashing at him mercilessly and stinging his back. Sy screamed and let go, falling into the darkness below.

Dawn was upon the Owens' farm. The morning sun rose over the hills. Patty gazed at the large tent, flapping in the light wind, then heard a scream within. She hesitated, unsure of what to do, and watched as the tent collapsed upon itself. Raising and lowering a few times as if someone or something was trying to get out, the tent began to swirl, the sides rising to touch each corner. The wooden poles holding the structure upright splintered and cracked, echoing like thunder off the hills. Then, the whole thing spun like a giant vortex until it disappeared into a large pit in the ground.

Patty had taken Sally and Eli to sit on the front porch of Mr. and Mrs. Owens' place. The couple had come back to their senses as soon as dawn peaked, the spell they were under apparently broken. Several townspeople, the ones who didn't get to the party in time, were wandering around the grounds, wondering why they were there and where their cars were.

Patty walked to the edge of the pit and looked in but saw nothing. She fell to her knees and cried.

The ground shook beneath her, and she watched in amazement as the pit began to shrink. Dirt from below filled the hole in the ground until it closed completely. The finality of it filled her with sadness, and she sobbed uncontrollably for the man she loved. The wind picked up, and she heard a voice from somewhere in the distance calling softly to her.

"Patty? Don't cry, baby. Mamma's here."

She saw a woman waving to her, motioning her to follow. The woman looked as though she were on a screen, some ancient black and white movie Patty had seen a hundred times before. Curiously, Patty walked toward her.

As she got closer, she realized she knew the woman, someone as familiar as herself. It was her mom.

"Mom? How?"

"Never mind how I got here. Patty, I was called to help you. What you seek is beyond the field. Sy's alive and trapped below. His people say so. There's an entrance over there." She pointed across the field in front of her. "Now, go to him. Help him."

"I will, Mom, but there's so much I want to say to you."

"Yes, I know, but we can't. I was summoned as a request to help you find him and nothing more." She slowly began to fade.

"No, wait. Mom, don't go." Patty watched as her mom disappeared.

Fresh tears filled her eyes, but there was nothing she could do. Sy needed her, and she'd go where her mom told her to.

When she reached the area on the other side of the field, Patty saw a large sinkhole in the ground and what looked to be a ledge with a ladder attached to it. She grabbed the top rung and placed her feet carefully onto the next one.

"I'm coming, Sy. Hold on."

She descended into the pit below.

Chapter Eighteen

Down Below

Opening his eyes, Sy knew, even in the darkness, where he was. The Pendleton Mine had a distinct smell. His back hurt. His legs hurt. Hell, everything hurt. Much like the times he dug the limestone from this pit.

He tried to stand, wincing from the pain as he put weight on his legs. One buckled, and he grabbed the wall to steady himself. He didn't think it was broken, maybe sprained. Either way, he'd have to endure if he were to get out of there. Only problem was, even though he knew he was in the mine, he had no idea what part he was in. Should he wait for help or try to find his way out? The darkness was impenetrable, no light coming from above. If he went forward, he risked the chance of wandering lost through an endless network of tunnels.

"Sy, go to the end of this corridor. There, you'll find what you're looking for." A dim light like a fuzzy television screen illuminated in front of him.

"Sadie? How is this possible? I saw you earlier, too."

"Don't fret on the how. When the parts come from hiding, so do the dead, some old and some new. But only for a time. Allen's on his own now. He has to find a way to rise above what he's become."

"What do you mean? What he's become? Is he someone else now?"

"He was, but he's seeing things the way they really are, and he's fighting against the evil trying to consume him."

"What can I do to help him?"

"Go to him. Support him. He's at the end of this corridor. He's going to need all the help he can get."

She faded from him. Oh, the things he wanted to say to her, but as she disappeared, he figured she'd accomplished what she came for, nothing more, nothing less.

Sy ran his hand along the wall and slowly made his way down the corridor until he saw a small sliver of light on the wall. It appeared to be coming from an opening. He turned his attention to it.

There was an area big enough for one person to get through, although it would be a tight fit. Sy could see a large chamber with lots of activity going on inside. Rebecca stood in the middle of the room, at least what used to be her. The tentacles were still present, but she'd become wrinkled and old. She looked alien, an octopus of some world Sy didn't know or want anything to do with.

Stranger still were the townspeople of Salt Flat and other people he didn't recognize, walking aimlessly about the chamber, their bodies falling into pieces then floating, trying to reattach. Ralph Oeny stumbled along with Tweedle-dee and Tweedle-dum, Rolo and Sam, close behind. Even in his state, he couldn't free himself of those two.

Others were present too. Henry McCarthy walked close to where Rebecca stood, his boys nowhere to be seen. He looked dazed, like someone sleep walking. The town grocer, Sam, milled about the room. Sy thought it strange to not see a smile on the man's face. He didn't remember seeing him during the revival, but there he was just the same. Buck Stanley walked close to him, talking to some guys Sy had never seen. They looked rough with lots of tattoos on their arms. One of the tats—it was hard to tell from that distance—looked like a naked lady.

Then, he saw one he didn't want to. His son-in-law, Tom, was among the bodies. Sally would be hurting over that one. The whole scene was disturbing. So many people he knew and took for granted seeing every day, all held in some trap they would never break free from.

Strangely, a blue flame fire burned in the center of the room, the same as in the tent during the revival. Beside it sat several large boxes with black lettering on them reading "MIXED PARTS". They lay scattered haphazardly around the flame. The big man, Samson he thought it was, stood near the boxes, gathering things from inside or putting them in. Sy couldn't tell in the dim lighting.

Sy looked for Allen but didn't see him. The Sage wasn't present either. What was it Rebecca said before the ghost appeared? He'd been compromised. Maybe they'd had a falling out? The whole thing was weird. Whatever the case, Sy needed out of there. Then, he could regroup, get some help, and find Allen. Although, he feared it might be too late for his son.

Another pressing problem was the ability to survive down there. The temperature was a good thirty degrees colder than outside. Back when he worked the mine, they would wear coveralls to protect from the elements. In jeans and a short sleeve shirt, he'd die of hypothermia before he ever got topside. He couldn't go into the chamber until everything was clear. He was in a jam. So distraught from his predicament, he failed to notice the figure coming from behind him.

"Hey."

Sy jumped at the sound of a female voice whispering in his ear. He let out a small yelp. The lady pulled him from the opening, placing a hand over his mouth.

He relaxed when he realized it was Patty, her other hand with her index finger in front of her lips. Sy nodded, and she released her hand from his mouth. They peaked into the chamber to make sure no one had heard.

"How'd you get here?" Sy whispered.

"I had help for part of the way. Then, I used the flashlight app on my phone for the rest, but its dead now, so I don't know how we'll find enough light to get out of here. That's all it was good for anyway. There's no service down here. Looks like we're fucked."

Secretly, he wondered if Sadie was around for her, too, but would save that question for later.

"Maybe not. I used to work down here, and if I remember correctly, the main mine shaft is on the other end of the big room in there." He pointed over his shoulder. "Only problem is, there's a lot of traffic between here and there. Also, I haven't seen Allen or that Sage fella come to think of it."

"What about Rhonda?"

"Nope."

"Can I take a look?"

Sy nodded and moved to the side so Patty could see inside the chamber. She craned her neck and gazed around the room to assess the situation.

"There's no way we'll get through there undetected. Is there an upper chamber?"

"Not that I'm aware of. This is the only way I know."

"I guess we need a distraction or something to get by them."

"I know. But what?"

As if to answer their question, the ground rumbled, and pieces of dirt fell from above. Inside the chamber, the townspeople screamed.

Sy and Patty looked through the small opening to see what the chaos was about.

Sepia toned light illuminated the large room as spirits began materializing near the top of the room, reminiscent of a movie projector starting the feature presentation. If it was, then it was sure to be a good show. Then a voice echoed.

"Behold, the one for which was foretold, the one who gives life eternal," Sage cried out. "I give you Rebecca!"

The spirits descended upon her and the mixed-parts people. Their bodies, having difficulty staying together already, burned and popped as their pieces fell and crawled on the ground, looking for a corner to hide. Spirits landed on Rebecca, and with what strength remained, she brushed them away. But it wasn't enough. She was shrinking, her feet sinking into the ground beneath her.

She screamed at Sage. "Why? Am I not enough for you? Why this betrayal?"

"I can tell you why. Because blood is thick here. My grandpa has come to see it, and so have I." Allen hovered beside Sage.

Grandpa? Sy thought. *Sage is related to them? But how?* His parents were dead and so were Sadie's as far as he knew. There was the story of one of her kin running off with a band of gypsies after he lost his daddy, but he would surely be dead by now.

Samson, stepping to the side of his queen, began pulling the spirits Calypso sent for Rebecca from her. His hands sizzled each time he touched one. Then, looking to Sage, his brow furrowed, and he began to hover. He picked up speed, heading straight for the man who invited the insult to his queen.

"You're weak, Sage, just like your father was!" Samson yelled.

Sage met his advance, and the two wrestled in the air, crashing into the top of the chamber, spraying rock and debris onto the floor below.

Allen flew to help him, but before he reached Sage, he was knocked sideways into the wall by one of Samson's arms. As weak as he was, as they all were, the large man still had something left in him. It would be a fight.

Rebecca fell to her knees and wept. Her body trembled as waves of agony gripped her. She sank further into the ground as a fresh wave of apparitions fell on her and the mixed-parts people. The ghosts circled Rebecca's people, the ones who were barely staying intact, corralling them toward her. The blue flame flickered and turned orange, then back to blue, unable to determine which way to go. The ground shook beneath the chamber as pieces of rock fell from the ceiling, crashing, and splintering on the floor. Sy pulled Patty toward him as a rock narrowly missed hitting her on the head.

"That was close. Thanks, Sy."

"This might be our chance, Patty. If we stay here any longer, we'll be buried with the rest of them."

"But what about Allen?"

"I want to help him, but I don't know how. Looks like he and Sage are taking on Samson. Until the fights over, there's not much we can do. You ready to go?"

She nodded and took his hand. Together, they stepped into the chamber. They eased along the wall, steering clear of the melee going on around them. They were halfway to the other side when they were confronted by an imposing figure.

Rhonda stood in their path, her body shaking, as though she were struggling to keep everything together. Her face was a maniacal menagerie of emotions, and she clearly wasn't pleased with what she was seeing. Another figure stepped from the shadows, one who struck fear in Patty's eyes the minute she saw him. Harley, as crazed and bloody as ever, struggling as much as Rhonda, stood ready to back her up.

"Hey, old man, bitch, where the fuck are you going?"

"Rhonda, don't you see what's going on here? Allen is lost to you. This whole place is going to fall in. We all need to get out of here," Patty said.

"No, I'm right where I need to be, among the parts and with my queen. We may not be strong enough to fight them," Rhonda said, pointing to the ceiling, "but we can take care of the likes of you. I'll rest with Rebecca soon, but before I do, I'll see to it you both die. I won't even think of making you part of Rebecca's hive. You lost your chance to live forever. The parts need to feed to make Rebecca strong. Now, move!"

Sy moved, as Rhonda and Harley pushed him, along with Patty, toward the middle of the room where Rebecca stood. Spirits moved around the chamber, occasionally hitting Rhonda and Harley. Harley snarled, smacking his body each time a fresh assault occurred, but Rhonda never flinched even though the look on her face was pure agony. Patty jumped sideways as another piece of ceiling fell between her and Sy.

"Looks like we're all going to be sealed in here," Harley said.

Sy gripped Patty's hand and pulled her close to him. If it was the end, he wanted to be next to her. For a second, he thought about how dying with her would be. *Would he see Patty and Sadie, together in his afterlife? Would they get along?*

He didn't have much time to ponder the situation. Harley pushed them to their knees in front of one of the boxes. As if sensing their presence, some of the parts came crawling out. Patty screamed as a bloodied stump of a hand worked its way up her leg, reaching for her midsection, clawing and groping. She attempted to stand but was forced back down by a laughing Harley.

"Take your fucking hands off her." Sy wriggled from Rhonda's grip, attempting to get to Patty.

Rhonda grabbed him by the shoulder, holding him in place. "Shut up, old man. It'll all be over soon."

More body parts streamed from the box, heading for Sy and Patty. Rebecca, her legs in the ground to her knees, turned her head toward them.

"Yes, my children. Feed on them me and make me strong."

Patty bucked her hips and sent the hand rolling from her, but others joined the fray. She squirmed against Harley's grip, trying to move away, but escape was impossible as he held her tight. Heads along with torsos, legs, and hands rolled from the boxes, wobbling along the ground, weakly trying to connect and get to the fresh bodies before them any way they could.

A head and torso of what appeared to be a woman managed to meld together in front of Sy, then looked curiously at him with glassy eyes. Blood and dirt lined her lips, and Sy watched in disgust as her mouth became wider with fresh rows of teeth cropping up instantly. In her weakened condition, she seemed to be having trouble finding him, chomping wildly in the air only inches from his face. Sy moved his head side to side to avoid her advances. Rhonda stooped behind Sy and held his head still.

"Don't move, old man., Wanda there is a friend of mine, and she needs some fresh blood." She looked at the parts as they haphazardly melded into cohesive bodies. "Feed on the feast we've prepared for you, my friends. Make Rebecca whole again!"

Patty cried out as a head bit into her leg. Sy turned his face from the partial woman and winced as her teeth grazed his skin. He looked at

Patty, the tears streaming from her eyes, Harley standing over her, his raspy laugh echoing throughout the chamber.

"Don't hurt her," Sy yelled.

"Quit your squirming, Sy. You'll find the pain only lasts for a minute." Rhonda jerked his head straight and nodded to the parts, encouraging them to make a fresh assault.

Wanda bit Sy's shoulder, and he snarled. The pain was intense, but his anger bore the brunt of it. Rhonda eased her grip, then breathed deep. Sy felt her body quivering as though she were enjoying his suffering, the experience bringing pure ecstasy. He noticed her grip loosening as she was caught in the throe's passion. So caught up in the throes of the passion, Rhonda relaxed her grip even further from Sy's shoulders.

Sy felt her grip loosen and seized the chance to get free. With all the strength he could muster, he threw his head back and smashed it into Rhonda's face. She reeled backward and fell onto her bottom. She reached for her nose, releasing her grip on Sy fully.

He jumped to his feet, nearly falling as his head throbbed from the impact to Rhonda's skull. He stumbled forward and managed to get a shoulder into Wanda's side, throwing her levitating torso into the rest of the parts, sending the few who'd managed to attach crashing into one another.

Harley threw Patty to the side and leaped for Sy, catching him in a football tackle around his midsection. They rolled across the floor, hitting the large wooden box, knocking the body parts coming over the top back into their dark tomb. The others ran into each other, confused at what was transpiring, like ants whose hill had been disturbed.

Sy tried to squirm free, but Harley's grip was too strong. Harley rose to his knees and straddled Sy, holding him firm on the ground with his outstretched arm. The crazed man's mouth widened, and Sy could hear his jaws cracking and popping as new teeth emerged from his gums.

A few inches from them, Patty rose to her hands and knees. The head attached to her leg had released her and was rolling on the ground, trying to find its way back to the tasty morsel of flesh it was working on. Patty grabbed it by the hair and picked the hideous thing up. She grimaced and watched as its teeth chomped crazily in the air, trying to get to her before throwing the head at Harley.

It connected with the side of his face. Harley, still holding Sy to the ground, flinched at the assault, then slowly turned his attention toward Patty.

"You, filthy cunt. Once I'm through with your boyfriend, you'll pay for that insult."

"Not before I rip your head off. Let go of him!" Patty, with fists raised, started for Harley. But before she could reach him, she was grabbed by the wrist and spun to see the wild-eyed face of Rhonda staring back at her.

"Nice try, but don't you all know when you're beat?" Blood dripped from her nose as her jaws opened wider.

Harley laughed, then turned his attention back to Sy. "Looks like we win, mate." Saliva dripped from his tongue and onto Sy's face.

Sy winced and turned his head as best he could, but not before the offensive ooze slid down his cheek. Harley placed a hand on Sy's head, pushing his face sideways and into the dirt. With his head to the side, he could see Rebecca, still held in her earthly trap. Wrinkled and shriveled, but not struggling as much.

Maybe after Harley and Rhonda were done, she would come back and hold her power over the town. He hoped not but didn't see it going any other way. The fight seemed to be lost. Sy wanted to look to the ceiling to see if Allen was still there, but it was useless. Harley held him tight.

Sy grimaced, waiting for the death blow. A sudden warmth invaded his body, comforting, like the touch of an old friend or lover. In his head, Sy heard a caressing voice, one he'd known most of his life.

"Don't worry, Sy, I've got this," Sadie said to him.

He smiled and relaxed as her spirit left him and entered Harley. The wild man released his grip and cried in agony as Sadie's' spirit wormed its way through his stomach, then throughout his body. Harley squirmed and fell backward, trying to free himself of the offensive thing inside him. He smacked his body like someone attacked by a hornet's nest, running into the wooden box and upsetting it.

The parts scurried out, looking for a new place to hide, but they had nowhere. Other ghosts were appearing, gathering the parts and burning them. The heads, mostly detached from their limbs, howled. Some of the parts rolled and dragged themselves back to the box, cowering inside.

Harley ran toward the flame and Rebecca, then he suddenly stopped, quivering in place. He reached for Rebecca, as a red flame from the fire in the middle of the room lashed out and caught him. He attempted to separate but couldn't. His body acted as though it didn't know what to do, a confused jumble of half in and half out pieces like a dynamic jigsaw puzzle. He howled and clawed at his face as the fire consumed him. His body exploded in a spray of blood and entrails, shooting in all directions from him.

Rhonda let Patty go and watched as Harley died.

Was he dead? How is it possible? Sy wondered.

Rhonda snarled as Sy rose to his feet. She ran towards him, fists raised, ready to rip him apart. He saw her coming for him and put out his hands, ready to take her blow, but none came. Rhonda stopped a few feet from him, dumbfounded by the sight in front of her.

A ghost stood there, flickering like an old television image. She had a baby attached to her breast; its bottom half gone.

"Nicole?" she said.

The spirit nodded, then entered Rhonda. Fire raced through her, a burning light dissolving her insides. She, as Harley did, tried to separate her body. But her efforts were for nothing. She was unable to move.

She slapped and clawed furiously at her skin. She tried to get the foreign invader from her but fell to her knees instead. Reality gripped her, and Sy watched as the realization dawned on her face. Sixty years was all she was afforded. She dragged her body toward Rebecca, and she cried out.

"My, queen! Save me."

It was the last thing Rhonda Lane would ever say.

The flame shot higher, red and orange hews replacing the blue light. Rebecca screamed, as did the rest of the parts, feeling the agony of their queen. The scene was pure chaos around the chamber, cries of anguish as the spirits continued their onslaught of the mixed parts. Trying to levitate, the parts fell in the dirt instead, unable to get the lift they needed. Rebecca was too weak to give them power.

Sy and Patty rose to their feet, watched as the parts wriggling. The smell of burnt flesh hung prominent in the air, like a large cookout, only the meat was spoiled. With the ghosts scattered in with their strange movie like appearance, Sy thought of an old Karloff silent picture he'd seen years ago on a television movie marathon. As he watched a detached hand crawling at his feet, he thought maybe more like a black and white zombie flick, but either way, he knew it was time for them to make their exit.

He squinted and tried to focus on the wall ahead, but with all the dust and smoke clinging to the stale air of the mine, it was hard to see anything. Finally, he did see something, hopefully what he was looking for, their escape route.

He pointed Patty in the same direction. "There it is. I think it's the opening I was talking about. It should lead to the main mine shaft."

They heard a large crash from somewhere above them. Sy hugged Patty to shield her from the rocks falling. Thankfully, it was small stuff, mostly dust, affecting their visibility but not hurting them. The light was dim as the flame in the middle of the room slowly died. Sy could barely make out anything, but he had to get them to the wall, to their only way out. He looked up and thought he caught a glimpse of Allen, but it was hard to tell. He'd worry about his son later. If he didn't get himself and Patty out of there right then, they'd be buried in the tomb forever.

But before they made it to the opening, a large rock fell from the ceiling, effectively closing off the area.

"Damn. There's got to be another way. C'mon, Patty."

Patty stopped him and pulled him close. "It's okay, Sy. You did your best. If this is it, we go down together." She looked him in the eye. "I love you."

Sy held her tight and began to cry. He'd always thought he'd only love one woman in his life, and he would have been fine if things turned out that way. But Patty, in some strange way, had worked her way into his heart and he was glad for it.

"I love you too," he said, then kissed her deeply as rocks and debris continued to fall around them, hitting, and pushing the couple to the ground until they were buried.

Chapter Nineteen

Awakening

Sy Sutton was driving down a lonely corridor of I-64, noticing the sky. *Red sky at night, a sailor's delight, red sky at morn, a sailor takes warn.* The same phrase he'd muttered to his children to allow them some comfort before a storm.

Sadie sat in the passenger seat. Allen and Sally were in the back, fighting and fussing about the usual things—who got the best toy from their Happy meal—when a large streak of lightning graced the darkness. The kids screamed.

"Dad, are we going to die?" Allen said, his sister swatting at him for saying such a thing.

Sy looked in the rearview mirror and smiled at his son, watching those innocent eyes pleading for some guidance. "No, son, we're not going to die. It's just God's fireworks, nothing to be worried about."

Allen smiled back, comforted in his dad's response. Taking Sadie's hand, Sy gave it a light squeeze. She returned the gesture, then crossed her hands and laid her head against the head rest, closing her eyes, trying to take a nap. Sy liked to watch her sleep, would even steal a glance her way to see her lovely head, the sight of her jaw line, nose, lips, all the things that made her perfect. She was a great mother, steadfast and caring in every sense. She was the perfect mate, and he could never imagine a day he wouldn't be with her, by her side, as they raised a family and grew old together.

Sy saw the storm getting worse. The clouds were stacked, a gray and black pillow rising into the heavens. He reached for Sadie's hand, but he became distraught. He couldn't find it.

She wasn't there.

Lightning streaked again, hitting the road, sparks fanned over the car, causing him to swerve. He looked in the rearview again, searching for Allen, knowing he'd need comforting once again. But instead of the boy who was there earlier, Allen was a man. He was mouthing words to Sy, but no sound was coming from his lips. Then muffled words appeared, phrases Sy couldn't hear clearly but read. The look on Allen's face was urgent, and Sy could tell he was yelling, the sound of his voice distant.

A crash outside snapped his gaze to the highway as bolts of electric tendrils streaked from the sky, connecting to the road in front of him at a greater frequency, causing huge plumes of fire to rise around the car. Sy, worried for his family, felt the urgency to get home quickly. But Sadie was gone; Sally was gone. Only Allen, the adult version, remained.

Sy felt Allen shaking him, so he let go of the wheel and turned to him. He watched his son mouth words to him, becoming louder until they were urgent cries.

"Dad! Wake up!"

Sy looked around and coughed. Allen stood next to him, covered in dirt, an unconscious Patty to the other side. He was in the chamber still, only a few steps from the opening. Allen was removing a large rock from his leg.

"Dad, this whole place is coming down. You and Patty need to leave, now."

Sy shook his head, trying to get his bearings. He nodded and attempted to rise to his feet, but he stumbled, catching himself on the rocks. Allen picked Patty from the mine floor as she was waking.

Sy could see the chamber on fire. A wall of flame shooting toward the ceiling had illuminated the place. Sy jumped as a head came barreling out of the flame toward him. He put his hands up in front of him and braced for the impact, but instead of hitting him, it burst in a fiery explosion, screaming a banshee cry as it did. The charred pieces of other body parts lay strewn across the floor, sizzling like eggs on a sidewalk in the summer heat. Allen put an arm around his dad and led him toward the opening. Still dazed, Sy watched as Sage was leading Patty to the same place.

"Allen? What happened? You were fighting the big man, then I lost track of you."

"Samson's subdued, hopefully gone forever with the rest of them."

"I love you, son, but I'm confused. Why the sudden change of heart?"

"I had a talk with Mom. Nicole too. They helped me see what was really going on. The lies Rhonda was telling. I was under her spell and Rebecca's too."

"I'm afraid I was under the same one, only much longer than my grandson," Sage said.

"When I heard you earlier, I thought you said something to that effect," Sy said.

"Yes. Sage is my great grandpa."

"Please, call me by my given name, Damien Reynolds. I almost forgot I was ever him."

"We had a talk before the revival started. Grandpa Damien betrayed his dad to be with Rebecca. Her idea of life eternal and strength beyond imagining appealed to him, but the price in the end was too high.

His soul became hardened. After Mom appeared to him, he softened, saw what was really important, his family. He saw me going down the same path and wanted to stop it before it was too late."

Sage smiled. "He's right. It took me an eternity to find such wisdom. The dead had come to me before, but I paid them no attention. It was like they were only in the background. It took my granddaughter to convince me. I had to call on an old enemy, who, I feel, is now a friend. I saw what was happening to Allen and didn't want to repeat it. Rebecca's way is enticing, but it takes your soul, making you nothing but an empty vessel. Her reign ends today."

"Dad, I'm sure you have a ton of questions."

"Son, I have more questions than I'll ever get answers for, but it doesn't matter, as long as you're okay."

"Yes, and I'm so glad you came to the chamber. Without your power feeding me and Grandpa Damien, we wouldn't have had a chance against Samson. Rebecca was trying to kill you, because she knew your strength, along with the rest of the family, would be her undoing. She failed though, and our family connection made it possible. You've always been there for me, and I'll never forget it."

"You're my son, and I'll never let you go it alone. Maybe after all this, we can have a long talk."

Allen released Sy to lean against the wall outside the chamber. "I'd like that very much." He nodded as Sage eased Patty to the floor next to Sy. They both turned for the room to join the melee again.

Sy grabbed for Allen's arm, stopping him. "Son, where are you going? You can't go back in there."

"I have to, Dad. We have to stop her. Samson is nearly defeated. He's weakened, anyway, and so is Rebecca. Now, we have to strike against her while she's in this state."

"She won't be for long. If she can gather the parts, she can become powerful again. Samson was trying to before the spirits intervened. Now, on their behalf and for the people of this town and all others she's stolen, we have to stop her. I've been Sage for the past one hundred years. Now, I must be Damien Reynolds again."

One hundred years? The man didn't look more than twenty at best.

Sy looked to Allen. "Will I see you again?"

"Maybe, Dad. If not in this life, then the next, but we'll see each other again, I'm sure," he said. "Dad? If I don't return, I'd like for you to do a favor for me."

"Sure, son, whatever you need."

"I have a daughter I didn't know about, somewhere in Lexington. Could you find her and give her a good home with her rightful family?"

"I have a granddaughter?" He looked at a smiling Patty, grabbed her, and pulled her close to him. He turned back to Allen. "It would be my honor."

Allen smiled, then looked at Sage. "C'mon, Grandpa Damien, let's do this." The two disappeared into the chamber.

On wobbly legs, Sy and Patty supported each other to standing and managed to move through the old mine shaft.

"You think he'll be all right?" she said.

"I don't know, but I have to have faith. He's a man, and he has to make his own decisions. I guess I need to let him go."

Patty pulled Sy close to her and kissed his dirty cheek. As they neared the opening to the mine, light peaking from the sun above, a large explosion rocked the earth beneath them, knocking them to their knees. They fell against the wall of the mine, unable to find the strength to go any farther. Dust rained down, covering them in a fine mist of particles. If Sy could hold her for the rest of his life, right there or anywhere else, he'd be satisfied, but before he became too complacent, he heard a ringing and something vibrating in his pocket.

It was his cell phone.

Sy fished it from its nest and smiled at the words on the display.

It was Sally.

The day after the revival was sunny with no clouds in the sky. A light breeze wafted through the town of Salt Flat. A few people meandered through the streets, trying to make it another day and forget the awful things they'd been through, the people they'd lost. But it was hard to do with so many reminders of the community that was there before.

Sam's IGA was closed, not even opened for its usual limited hours on Sunday. Sam didn't make it in as he had every morning for the previous thirty years. The Methodist church was also closed with Pastor Mooney nowhere to be found. His associate pastor gave assurances it would be open the next week and for Wednesday services if enough showed up.

Carla Williams, the only law officer left in the town, tried to put the sheriff's office back together and bring some semblance of security but feared it was no use. Until they installed a new sheriff, the people would be fearful. Who could blame them? She'd notified the state police about the situation and was assured they would send investigators, but that was of little consolation to the people of the town.

One of the greatest tragedies of all was the loss of so many parents. Children who were with sitters and relatives the night of the revival woke to news their moms and dads wouldn't be coming home. Sally Chambers stepped in to help, as did her dad, Sy, and his new girlfriend, Patty. She was a welcome addition to the tattered community. As a nurse, she had some much needed skills.

Salt Flat suffered some great losses the night of the tent revival, and it would be a while before it healed, if ever. But heal it must. The town had to go on, even if its citizens were mostly gone. A sickness had invaded, and the ominous presence would remain for many years to come. If it was to go forward, it would be up to the children to make it happen.

Later in the week, the state police took all the reports they could, starting at the Owens' farm. The owners stood by their story of nothing happening on their farm, to the police and the various news reporters who'd descended on the area, in spite of all the abandoned cars, most of which belonged to the missing townspeople. The police did find a motor home parked about thirty miles from Salt Flat in a state park. The registration couldn't be tracked as it didn't exist. Then there was the damage from a suspicious crack in the earth going from the Owens' farm to the Pendleton mine where a large sinkhole remained, the same one a man from town had fallen into about a few months before.

At the request of the state, geologists came in to study the area. They found peculiar readings and burns in the rock. One of them thought they saw a rock moving down at the bottom of the crater. Well, maybe not. It wasn't in the official report, but the story around town and at Pa-Rudy's bar was they did see something. Stories told by drunken patrons. The stuff legends are born from.

Eventually, workers came in and bulldozed the sinkhole in an attempt toto cover it up. They gave up after suffering equipment failures and the near loss of a man whose dozer was buried in the earth forever. It seemed the sinkhole and crack in the ground would remain as a reminder of what happened in Salt Flat and how the people were duped into believing in false prophets.

A month or so after the tent revival, another of Salt Flat's long-time residents, Sy Sutton, had disappeared, but there was nothing nefarious about those circumstances. He left town for a while, on a road trip with a pretty nurse by the name of Patty Hudson. But first, the pair would make a stop in Lexington, KY to hunt down a certain someone who they hoped would be a welcome addition to the family. The day they left, both were smiling.

EPILOGUE

On a stretch of highway somewhere Northeast of Kentucky, a Cadillac Fleetwood, the kind you'd see in some presidential cavalcade, sped along with a large truck beside it. Earlier, a motor home was with them but was left abandoned in a local park, as it was no longer needed. The truck's destination was to the New York area in some undisclosed warehouse. The drivers of the truck knew nothing of the cargo, the way Samson intended it to be. The large man made no mention of the boxes with "Mixed Parts" painted on the side. He only instructed the delivery man to be careful. All had to be done quickly, as time was of the essence. Taking a puff of his inhaler, the breath long and deep, he continued to drive.

Samson supposed he was lucky to be driving at all. The whole situation in the mine had gone so wrong. Rebecca was reduced to nothing more than a shell of her former self, her power greatly diminished, the collection of souls down to only a couple of boxes.

The spirits had turned vengeful. He figured it was only a matter of time. Rebecca warned of it. The dead had turned on her before. Usually, when the parts came to life, they only took a few to be appeased, then left the rest to Rebecca. But that time, like a hundred years before, was different. If Sage hadn't supported them, hadn't invoked the name of her mortal enemy, maybe they would have let Rebecca thrive, then her power would have no end, but who knew? The dead were so unpredictable.

At least with Sage and Allen gone, he'd be Rebecca's main general again. Why they turned to the spirits, he'd never know. They could have had life eternal with Rebecca. But instead, they released the fury of the dead and brought forth Calypso, destroying most of the parts in the process.

Calypso? The very one he and Sage defeated all those years before. Samson supposed they intended to destroy Rebecca as well, but he took care of them, fighting the pair to the point of exhaustion. He'd thought they would finish him, but instead they withdrew, disappearing into the red flame. Maybe Calypso couldn't go any further? Didn't have as much power as they thought? He didn't know.

Afterward, the ghosts came for him, but he'd been thinking ahead. He had an escape route, a bubble the spirits couldn't find. He'd squirreled away three boxes in a hidden part of the mine filled with holy ground dirt from the local cemetery. Rebecca had told him many years ago the dead couldn't find you in the soil they'd come from. He'd grabbed his queen and whatever parts he could find while enduring the insults of the ghosts burning him.

Once he had all he could carry, Samson put them, as well as himself, in the boxes. After a couple days' sleep, he woke and got in touch with his benefactors to arrange a pick-up. By that time, the ghosts were gone, back to whatever hole they'd come from, the parts no longer buzzing with life for them to attach to. For his selfless act, Rebecca gave him the last of her strength to make him whole again. With it, he managed to get her and the boxes out of the mine.

But in her condition, Rebecca would need to stay hidden for a while longer. The warehouse would be temporary until he could get her to a place somewhere away from the city. Then, the parts would join her later when she was ready.

In a few hours, they reached their destination, a warehouse in Brooklyn, owned by the Pendleton Corporation. The gate opened and a security guard motioned them in. Samson stepped from the Cadillac and greeted a woman in a sensible suit with a white name tag as bright as her smile reading "Stephanie". He took a breath from his inhaler, then tucked it in his pocket.

"Samson, good to see you again. I hope your trip was uneventful?"

"No problems, other than the mine incident."

"Yes, we heard. Will this delay things?"

Samson sighed. "Most likely, at least until she's ready again. Do you have the storage facility prepared?"

"Why, yes. Mister Pendleton was specific about the way everything should be done. An underground location, free of outside lights, only a propane heater, although with the temperature down there and the fact it's summer, I don't foresee any heating issues."

"Do not concern yourself with it. I'll see to the storage of the boxes."

"Well, okay, I guess. I'll make sure Mister Pendleton is notified once you are inside."

"Good. Do you have people looking for a suitable residence outside the city, one less conspicuous than here?"

"Yes, I have my people checking now. Where is the other fellow? Sage, I believe it is? Will he be joining you later?"

"No, he met with an unfortunate event and is no longer with us."

"A shame. I liked the Sage. He had a certain charm I found appealing. I trust many new converts were brought into the collective? Mister Pendleton raves about your church services. The people dying to save their souls. Maybe I should come see them sometime?"

Samson smiled, taking a puff from the inhaler, the device popping when it left his mouth. "You'd be a welcome addition. Maybe when we get settled?"

"Good, I'll take you up on the invitation. Now, if you'll pull up to the building, I'll have the guard open the door."

The truck lumbered forward through the large open door with Samson close behind in the car. Once inside, they drove to the lowest level of the building. The truck's air brakes hissed as they descended the ramp. The stark gray walls and fluorescent lighting gave a cave like appearance to the place, perfectly suitable. Once the lights were out, it would be like the mine. As Stephanie had said, the blue flame, via the propane heater, sat in the middle of the room. Large shelves, big enough for several tons of cargo, adorned the walls on either side of the room and stretched on forever it seemed. They wouldn't need so many, only a few as the boxes numbered less. It saddened Samson to see it, but they would rebound. He knew his queen was resilient.

The truck came to a stop near the middle of the room, and the workers hopped out, quickly going to the back. They opened the cargo door and slid the conveyor ramp from its nest, easing it to the concrete floor. Samson shut the car off and stepped out. His six-foot-ten height and large frame gave him an imposing advantage when instructing others, and the workers were clearly nervous as they waited for his instructions.

"Remove the wooden boxes and place them on the shelves near the middle of the room. There is one that will look different from the others. Place it on the floor and await my return. I'm going up a level to ensure everything is secure."

The men nodded their understanding and got to work as Samson disappeared into a nearby stairway.

Once the boxes were in their place, all except for the odd one, the workers rested, sitting on that particular box until the big man came around to give them further instructions. One of the men pulled a pack of cigarettes and a lighter from his pocket. He tapped the pack and one dropped part way from the box. He grabbed it with his dried lips and lit it, the orange flame glowing in the dim lighting. The cigarette glowed bright red as he drew in, smoke disappearing into the man's mouth and nostrils as he inhaled. It rolled into the air once he breathed a satisfying exhale.

"Hey, Charlie? Did anybody tell you what was in these boxes?"

"Naw. I don't ask questions, just do the job. These fuckers are paying good, so, why ask, Al?"

"I don't know, seems a little odd is all. What's with the guy who hired us? Talk about your weirdos. Guy gives me the creeps. Fucker's big enough to bench press both of us."

"I know, Al. I wish he'd get here soon. I want to get my drinkin' money and get to partyin'."

"What's up with this one?" Al tapped on the box, ashes falling from the tip of the cigarette onto the binding. He brushed them away, leaving a light gray stain on the pale leather.

"What do you mean? It's just an old box."

"Naw, Charlie. This looks like something those Mexican cartel guys use. You know, the guys who make boots out of human skin. I seen a pair of those once. Guy I was drinkin' with down in Hell's Kitchen. He said he had the guy killed, and then they gave him the boots, so he'd know the asshole was dead. I didn't believe a word of it, but after seeing this box, I don't know."

"Fuck off, Al. There ain't no way that's skin covering that thing. Hey, can I bum one of those from you?"

Al tapped out another cigarette and handed it to Charlie. Flipping the lighter wheel, the butane fueled canister glowed to life, the orange flame illuminating Charlie's face in the dimness of the room.

"What are you doing?!"

The men jumped to attention. Samson stood there with an unpleasant look on his face.

"Why are you producing flames? Do you know how fragile this cargo is?"

Charlie spoke up. "Sorry, man, we didn't think about it. We'll put them out."

Charlie threw his cigarette to the ground and stepped on it, moving his foot back and forth to extinguish the burning tip. Al puffed out his chest in a defiant gesture, then flipped his cigarette to the side. Cinders fell over the leather bound box as it bounced a couple of times before hitting the floor. But instead of smashing it like Charlie did, Al let it burn.

"There, happy now?"

Samson smiled, his gaze not on the man who was insulting him but, on the box, where a reddish, rope-like tentacle was working its way from the partially open top. It eased down the side, wrapping around Al's ankle. Al's eyes widened as he saw the alien thing attached to his leg.

"The fuck?" He was upended, falling with a thud on his back.

He screamed while other tentacles wrapped around him. Samson then watched as Charlie shook his head, trying to make sense of what was transpiring. Nervously stumbling backward, the man fell to his knee, the apparent pain sending shock waves through his leg. But he ignored it and launched into a run for the stairway.

Samson laughed so hard he started to cough. He pulled his inhaler from his pocket and took a breath, producing a popping sound when it released from his lips. Gurgled sounds of protest were coming from Al as he disappeared into the box, tentacles stuffed in his mouth, working down his throat.

"Looks like Rebecca has paid you in kind for your recompense," Samson said, then threw his arms to the air in a triumphant gesture, releasing them from his body.

Charlie made it to the door, but as he tried to turn the handle, he was stopped. A big arm with no body attached to it had him by the wrist. Blood curdled screams came from the young man as another arm descended into his chest. The pain was sudden but subsided quickly. He could feel the hand inside him grasping for something.

He blinked as he saw his own heart beating in front of him for a second until he collapsed, face first on the floor.

Samson's arms returned to him with the pulpy, bloody organ in his hand. Samson ate it and smiled as he heard the young man stir. He smirked as Charlie stepped clumsily toward him, his body like a marionette puppet. Samson watched the boy curiously.

"Your friend wasn't pure enough to be part of the hive, but you will make a nice addition. Are you worthy of immortality?"

The young man nodded his head. Samson knew Charlie felt no pain. As a matter of fact, he would never feel more alive!

End

ALSO BY

EDMUND STONE

Books

The Rebecca Mythos

Tent Revival

The One

Lost Hope

The Within Series

Within: A Three Part Horror

Punish: The Sequel to Hurt

Delilah: The Sequel to The Devil's Concubine

Collections

Blues, Blood, and Love

Hush My Little Baby

Collaboration

The Little Runaway

with Patrick Reuman

ABOUT THE AUTHOR

Edmund Stone is a writer of horror and suspense, and a part time boat captain. He resides in a home along the Ohio River with his wife, four dogs, and a group of mischievous cats. He is the author of six books and two short story. He has several short stories residing in various anthologies as well. His books can be found on Amazon and a few independent sellers.

Find him at edmundstoneauthor.com or at https://linktr.ee/edmundstoneauthor

edmundstoneauthor.com

Contact him at riverrevivalpress@gmail.com While on edmundston
eauthor.com, be sure to sign up for my newsletter to get a free story
and all the latest information on new releases from Edmund Stone
Author.